The Darden Pursuit

Brad Argiro

This book is dedicated to all of those we have loved
and lost...thanks for watching over us!

ACKNOWLEDGMENTS

Creating a book from an idea is truly a labor of love. I have many people to thank along the way including:

My wonderful wife- You are the love of my life, my best friend, my partner in crime. I feel blessed every day that you chose me, and I love our life together!

My son Anthony- I couldn't ask for a better kid and you're the smartest guy I know!... Hope I had just a little bit to do with that!

My family- The Argiros and the Prohovics. The Argiros have had to put up with me my whole life, the Prohovics not quite as long. Both families are incredibly supportive, generous, and always there to lean on… Love you all!

My friends- Few things in life are as rewarding as true friendship and I treasure you my friends!

Thanks again everyone…this was fun!

1

He crouches silently in the bushes across the parking lot from the convenience store. Staring at the window, watching the heads of customers and employees milling about inside, he hums to himself an unrecognizable tune and waits for his prize. He times the tune to the occasional swoosh of a passing car on the highway behind him, imagining the sound to be that of cymbals crashing. A pleasant accompaniment to his imaginary orchestra, he further imagines a far-off barking dog to be a bass drum…a blowing horn a trumpet…the sound of the warm breeze passing through the bushes just like a woodwind. He is unaware of where his musical talents come from, where almost everything that makes up his life comes from for that matter. The talent is there though, undeniably, and his creativity abundant. Some would say wasted, misguided talent, but he has no use for others and their stupid opinions. He is his own man...his own God...and he believes only in himself.

Tonight, as he waits to do what must be done, the killer is not a killer. He is instead a brilliant composer of art. Tonight, in his mind, he is Mozart, Beethoven, or Tchaikovsky. Until the time comes, whenever that may be, he will wait. He will do what he came to do on this hot and humid August night because that's the way it must be. He is God...he is his own savior...he is...as his mind drifts away again, he hears the swoosh of another passing car from the highway...crashing cymbals...and he goes back to composing his masterpiece.

He has almost completed the first movement of his imaginary symphony when it starts. First, on the underside of his right forearm, radiating to the base of his hand...a burning, gnawing, and all-to-familiar itching. It seems to dig into the depths of his very soul, causing him to shake so violently that he imagines his bones rattling together and making a noise like wet wood crackling in a burning fire. Just when he can stand the torment no longer, succumbing to his misery by standing and exposing his camouflaged position…the car he is waiting for arrives

The man who emerges from the vehicle is handsome and appears to be in his forties. He is tall but not awkwardly tall, perhaps six feet, dark hair with just a hint of gray at the temples. He is slick and dapper in appearance with the upper class, high profile look of a big time. He wears a dark sports jacket which compliments his equally dark trousers and dress shoes. His movements display the certain elegance and refinement of perhaps a high-level executive. The appearance of the target only fuels the agitation of the killer. As the man approaches the convenience store, he initiates a tirade of insults against him under his breath. "Who are you, asshole? Who do you *think* you are?" His quiet knifing of the businessman continues…"I know who *you* are…do you know who *I* am?…you are going to find out who I am!!" Now the itching intensifies, and his agitation becomes a storm of outrage. Cursing to himself again, he reaches his trembling hand into the pocket of his zip-front jacket, brushing his hand on the cold metal of the revolver.

The businessman has entered the store, unaware of the leering eyes that follow him. The killer gathers his strength and rises slowly from his crouched position in the bushes. Quickly he must act, despite the growing sensation that control is slipping from him under an avalanche of suffering. Drawing upon all the strength he can muster, he moves stealthily behind one parked vehicle, then another...moving slowly closer to the black SUV. Then a moment of panic as a younger man exits the convenience store and strolls into the parking lot.

For a moment, he seems to be heading directly for him, reaching for something in his pocket. The killer grabs for his revolver. His head spins as he tries to assess his situation. He would have nothing against eliminating this unexpected intruder. Human life is meaningless to him. They are of no more significance than an insect on the sidewalk...an annoying inconvenience. He hesitates though, reluctant to draw attention and endanger his mission. The young man produces from his pocket a cell phone. He quickly dials then looks up, his eyes scanning the parking lot. Seconds seem like hours as the killer fears he has been spotted and his lethal plan thwarted. Has the man seen him, grown suspicious, and decided to call for help? The killer's pulse races, his thoughts now spinning wildly as he struggles to assess his plight. Finally, he watches with a rush of relief as the young man's eyes lock on a vehicle several feet away. He has merely been searching for his own car. With renewed calm, the killer watches as the young man, engrossed in his phone conversation, starts his car and heads for the highway. Only seconds after the vehicle disappears into the blackness of night, the businessman emerges from the store…stepping briskly in the direction of his parked SUV…and his date with death.

The killer attempts once again to calm himself and to draw upon his inner strength. He steadies himself by focusing his rage on his target…distracting himself from the growing sensation that his burning skin is now swarming with insects burrowing deeper inside of him. "Now or never!!…Now or never!!" he mutters to himself…"I am my own God!!…I am my own savior!!" As the businessman continues his approach, the killer steps suddenly from behind the SUV, shaking violently with revolver in hand. As he comes upon his nemesis, a look of bewilderment appears in the businessman's eyes…as if pondering a riddle or a puzzle that he will never have time to solve. Suddenly, an explosion of gunfire…a horrific scream of pain and terror…then darkness.

2

Matthew Darden sits motionless and stares at the blinking cursor of his computer screen. A prisoner in a world of daydreams and night terrors, he lives a lonely and isolated life. Writing is the creative outlet for Matthew, a blessing to his otherwise meaningless existence…an escape from his pain and a temporary sedative to calm his fears. Though often an escape from his misery, writing sometimes brings him to a dark and horrible place. A place where the forgotten demons of his past seem to reach for him, imploring him to join them in their dance of darkness.

Matthew suffers from a condition known as Dissociative Amnesia, a state that occurs when a person blocks out certain information, usually associated with a stressful or traumatic event. The condition robs him of his identity and much recollection of his past. Although more than three years have passed since the one event that would forever alter his existence, his condition remains the same. His case is rare and seemingly hopeless. Amnesia is not always a permanent condition. Some individuals, with the help of a strong support group, intense psychotherapy, and proper dosage of medication can improve. Some may even regain bits of memory over time, breaking through the imaginary walls that surround them to reconnect with family and friends. This can never be the case with Matthew Darden, a man cut off from the world and completely detached from reality. Although limited, memories do appear to Matthew…sometimes in frantic, fast-moving frames of light and sound that rouse him from sleep, reducing him to child-like screams. Sometimes more pleasant visions appear to him in flowing strands of pleasurable sights and sounds that stir in him a yearning to remember and rejoice. Often, he plants these visions in his writings. His works are sometimes hopeful and beautiful, other times, disturbing or altogether incoherent. Tonight, sitting at that small workstation in his one-bedroom apartment, his mind is blank. Unable to conjure up a single written word, he continues to stare mindlessly at the blank monitor and brush his scruffy beard. Listening to the hum of the small fan perched on his nightstand, he begins to feel the walls closing around him.

Matthew places his hand on his chest and feels the furious pounding of his heart. Beads of sweat appearing on his forehead, he starts to sob for no clear reason. Breathing becomes increasingly difficult as his throat begins to narrow, and his chest begins to tighten. Now in the throes of a massive panic attack, Matthew lifts himself from his chair, his feet now two lead weights supporting his quivering body. Slowly, he makes his way to the twin bed in the far corner of the room. He throws himself upon it, as if having been hurled from a ten-story building. His heart pounding as if about to leap from his chest, he lays face up on the mattress, listening to the relentless pounding of his heart and sobbing continuously. From the window closest to the bed, he can hear the voices of the summer tourists on the streets below…passing beneath his window, loose on the streets of Wildwood, New Jersey…voices of the late-night party crowd growing ever louder in their search for the nearest bar and next drink. Matthew, still in his state of panic and unable to bear the sound of the revelry, covers his ears with his hands and begins to mutter out loud, quietly at first…"leave me alone…leave me alone." Anger begins to take hold of him, and his mumbles turn into furious shouts…LEAVE ME ALONE!!…LEAVE ME ALONE!!…his trembling hands still pressed firmly against his ears. Sweat dampens his dark hair as he moves his head back and forth on the pillow. He pleads for reprieve from his miserable state and hopeless thoughts. Mercifully, fatigue begins to take hold of his body as he slowly succumbs to sleep. Finally, willing to close his eyes, Matthew Darden crosses over into the land of dreams…and nightmares.

He could see the car's dashboard and headlights of the oncoming traffic through the blurriness of the rain-soaked windshield. He could hear the screams …his own screams at first…then the screams of a woman and child. Upside down…the hum of the idling motor still present in his eardrum…the smell of gasoline, smoke, and…oh God!!…burning skin. Water on his face and raindrops running through the broken windows. The taste in his mouth…the awful taste of his own blood. His head pinned, trying to utter the words…"are you there?"…"please answer me…please answer me"…"please don't leave me here alone." Sirens approaching in the distance…the feeling that he may wretch…"close your eyes now"…"just close your eyes." A man standing over him…a man in a white coat…bright lights above and around him…the man is talking to him…talking too much to him. The man is telling him that he must believe…he must stay strong. "I am your only hope" says the man, "and you are mine."

Matthew Darden leaps from the bed with blaring screams. Tripping over the nightstand, the small fan falls to the wooden floor with a crash. Sweat pours from his forehead and his entire body shudders in unison. He swivels his head from side to side, scanning the room on either side of him and behind. As if fighting some invisible creature, he flails his arms helplessly. Believing he is no longer in his bedroom, but transformed somewhere, in some other time…locked in a cold, dark place with something evil lurking. He reaches for the light switch, hoping the light will bring some comfort and recognition. The light only brings his disheveled room back into view. The sweat-soaked mattress of his bed and the small fan lying on the floor. Books and pencils are scattered about, knocked around during his tussle with the unseen malevolence. Matthew begins to feel his muscles slowly beginning to loosen and his pulse returning to a normal pace.

He steps carefully around the clutter and heads down the hallway toward the bathroom. He flips on the bathroom light switch and stares at himself in the mirror. He turns on the water and splashes cool water in his face, hoping this will revitalize him. He cups his hands under the faucet and brings the cool, sweet water to his parched lips. As Matthew continues to stare intently into the mirror, he becomes upset again. His despair is not due to the sight of his tired eyes, graying hair, or the deep worry lines on his forehead. As he stares at his reflection, a dreadful thought occurs to him…he doesn't even recognize the face staring back at him. Too distraught to switch off the bathroom light, Matthew wanders back into his bedroom. He paces around the room as if he is a caged animal…searching high and low for an exit from the walls which confine him. To occupy his whirling mind, he sits back down at his computer. Without thought, he begins to type…his mind no longer a blank slate…words beginning to come to him.

The mindless humans bathe in the warm, inviting darkness…unaware of the heartless and savage creatures swimming among them…

Without warning his writing is interrupted again. This time by a feeling…an impulse. Something draws him to the other window on the opposite side of the bedroom…the one that overlooks the small alleyway on the side of the apartment complex. As he moves to the window and slowly lifts the shade, a chill comes over him. A feeling of dread that he cannot comprehend…the cold, black feeling of death. As he stares down the alley, he spots a dark figure staring up at him. Matthew's stomach drops…hairs standing on end now. For a moment his eyes lock on the figure and he can discern that it is a male. The reflection of the light from inside the apartment makes it difficult to tell…but it is a male…he is sure of this. He is unable to fully discern the features of the man before he turns the corner and disappears. Matthew Darden is left alone again with his thought and fears...and the feeling that whether in dream or reality...he has seen this man before.

3

The afternoon sun bakes the Atlantic City Boardwalk as a warm summer breeze blows off the ocean. A mob of humans consisting of everyone from Millennials , junkies, to elderly gamblers strolling from one casino to another. In and out of the revolving doors of huge hotels, tripping over each other to spend their tax refunds, disability checks, social security, and 401k's. A middle-aged drunk man stumbles along, yelling at his wife…teenage girls carrying bags full of the latest fashions from the trendy stores of the popular Pier Shops…an armless and legless woman lies on the boardwalk. She plays a keyboard for quarters…oblivious to the taunts of the crowd moving by. This passes for a typical afternoon in Atlantic City, the famous gambling Mecca of the East. A city to which the wealthy and poor...the beautiful and ugly...the lucky and the cursed are drawn like bees to a hive. A city where money is made and lost...where dreams are born and die.

The killer watches this fascinating human spectacle from a park bench on the ocean side of the boardwalk. Behind his dark sunglasses, he scans the crowd for the moment...enjoying the show of everyday life carrying on around him. To pass the time, he sings quietly to himself a tune that fits the occasion...a line from a Bob Dylan song though he can't recall the title...

"Atlantic City by the cold gray sea...I hear a voice crying daddy, I always think it's for me..."

He taps his foot to the beat of an imaginary drum, singing to the rhythm of the crowd noise and squeaking wheels of the human taxis pushing passengers in covered carts to their next destination. He derives pleasure from being this close to them, watching them. He thinks about how lucky these lost souls are to be in the presence of him...to be within reach of his talents and wisdom.

How they would worship him if they knew who he was and what he was. They would fall on their knees and praise him if they knew. With the activities of the afternoon carrying on around him, he glances at his wristwatch…feeling only a faint tingling on the underside of his forearm…it's almost time.

Satisfied that the appropriate time has come, the killer rises from the park bench and heads in the direction of the casino. Waiting his turn at the door and resisting the urge to force his way through the congestion of the crowd, he enters the gaming floor. Past the steady whistling of the slot machines…past the cashiers and the blackjack tables…scanning the room and formulating his plan. He pauses momentarily to soak in his surroundings, marveling at the sights and sounds around him. The casino itself is a wonder to behold with beautiful gold railings encircling bright red carpets. Two sports cars spin on giant display racks, enticing visitors to spend their coins for the chance to drive home a winner. Two large escalators, also trimmed in gold, transport hotel guests from the casino floor to elegant accommodations upstairs. He pauses to watch the crowd gathered around the roulette wheels and craps tables, delighting at the cheers and sighs from the winners and losers. He turns his attention from the floor to the detailed ceiling and brilliant chandeliers hanging from it. He also takes note of the several black bubble-like glass structures pointing at the tables below. He recognizes these objects as security placements, the so called "eyes in the sky". He is fully aware that each of these bubbles houses a camera which feeds dozens of monitors. He knows that in a room not far from where he is standing, a trained staff studies these monitors. He reminds himself that he must avoid detection…he must act wisely, and he must not falter. He senses that the time is drawing near now, the tingling in his forearm becoming more pronounced and sweat beads beginning to form on his forehead.

Looking down at his wristwatch again, the killer becomes increasingly impatient. He feels as if a typhoon is brewing inside of him. He grows increasingly more agitated by each passing second, losing his composure to the inexorable itching that is now impossible to ignore. Trying to settle himself now, he begins to plead with his body…"hold on, just hold on"…"Dammit!!...hold on just a little longer!" He has also drawn the attention of a uniformed security guard who moves toward him with growing suspicion. He again attempts to steady himself…this time by grabbing his quaking right hand with the left to appear casual. The security guard doesn't buy the routine and in a curt tone asks if there is a problem. "No problem, I just need to find a restroom" is the killer's reply. The security guard points brusquely to the far end of the room and the killer walks hastily away from the confrontation. He can't see the eyes of the security guard following him, though he is sure they are there. He moves through the casino, up a small ramp, past a row of vending machines to the restroom. His head is spinning, and his skin is crawling…he is running out of time.

Standing at the row of sinks and staring at his reflection in the large mirror of the restroom, he focuses on his breathing to calm himself. He waits for an elderly man to finish his business at the urinal and tries to block out the happy whistling of another man washing his hands beside him. He notices that this man is studying him out of the corner of his eye. "What the hell are you looking at?" the killer says to himself but not out loud. Who is this stranger to stare at him?…to judge him. He fantasizes about how he could dispose of this nosy waste of humanity. He could grab him and choke him right here, right now. He could bash his head off the of the sink, splattering his brains on the bathroom floor. The man turns away from the sink and walks out the door, the elderly man follows behind him. "Today is your lucky day" the killer mutters out loud this time. He is alone again, studying his face in the mirror…the face of a monster.

The deep breathing technique at the mirror, along with a few splashes of water, have at least somewhat soothed his condition. At least for the moment, he feels more in control. The itching in his arm has settled into a numb, tingling feeling. The sweat on his forehead has dried somewhat and he has an easier time controlling his balance upon walking. He is encouraged by this new sensation. He senses that his body is slowly changing…evolving…becoming an even more perfect machine. He exits the casino restroom with a renewed sense of purpose…a determination to complete his task. He steps out once again onto the gaming floor. He scans the room in search of the security guard, darting his eyes across a sea of gamblers. With the guard seemingly nowhere in sight, he feels safe to proceed. He turns and walks in the direction of a sign at the far end of the casino…the one that reads "Piano Bar".

Entering the piano bar is a stark contrast to the intense and raucous atmosphere of the casino. The room is much more subdued in both appearance and attitude. Instead of the brilliant, bold colors of the casino, The Piano Bar is dimly lit and intimate. The tables and booths are filled mostly with couples. There is a lot of hand holding and cuddling as the audience sways to the soothing sounds of mellow music. The killer stands at the entrance and quickly scans the crowd before selecting an unoccupied table near the rear of the room. This selection of table allows him full view of both the customers and talent. He watches with interest as the musician sits at the black Steinway piano, his fingers moving effortlessly through a nice rendition of an Elton John song. A waiter approaches to take his order. Needing to blend in, but weary of introducing alcohol to his system, the killer orders a tonic water instead. He sips the drink and occupies his time by listening to the music and studying the crowd. His attention turns to an attractive young couple at the table next to him. The man rests his hand in the woman's lap, she lays her head on his shoulder. The scene feels somehow familiar to the killer though he can't comprehend why. He is confused by this sudden emotion, a lump forming in his throat, his eyes beginning to moisten. He chastises himself under his breath, redirects his thoughts, and reminds himself that he must stay ready and alert. His eyes return to the musician at the piano, where it remains for the final few songs of the evening. As the pianist closes with "Let it Be," the killer begins to feel the sensation returning to his forearm. He moves to his feet as the musician bows to applause and exits to the dressing room…the hunt is on.

He waits at the entrance to the skywalk, a glass enclosed walkway with a flat escalator which runs over a parking lot below. These escalators transport visitors from the casino to the Pier Shops, a three-story mall built on a pier extending into the Atlantic Ocean. He stares through the glass at the parking lot below, reminding himself to relax and breathe deeply. The itching has returned now, along with the sweating. He feels he is losing control once again. He stands with his feet firmly planted to the floor, hands in both pockets to disguise the shaking. He studies each face moving past him. He makes eye contact with several of them and their eyes move quickly away from his menacing stare. He is convinced that they are merely in awe of him...they sense his power and complete control over them. What a wonder he must be to behold...how small they must feel to him. If they knew, they would not be walking along concerned about their clothes, their looks, or their money. They will of course know him in time, he tells himself. They will all know him, and they will run from him...but he will find them...he will find all of them in time. Tonight however...he waits for only one.

Eventually he spots him...heading for the escalator...heading right for him. The musician from the piano bar is wearing dark sunglasses and has changed into a bright-blue silk shirt and blue-jeans. Although small in stature, he carries himself as if he is much larger. He walks along arrogantly, moving through the crowd and stopping for no one. He appears to be in his mid-thirties with a thin build and dark, thinning hair. He breezes by the killer, leaving the scent of cheap cologne in his wake. He is unaware he is being followed. Across the skywalk and into the entrance of the mall...past the information booth and onto another escalator. The killer follows him, staying several paces behind to avoid detection. He waits as the musician enters a Starbucks, emerging moments later with a large, Styrofoam cup of coffee. He follows him as he pauses outside a clothing store, admiring a leather jacket hanging in the window. The musician then heads for the rear exit of the mall at the end of the pier. He reaches into the pocket of his blue jeans and pulls out a pack of Camel Cigarettes. He opens the glass doors and steps out into the darkness to enjoy his cigarette and the view of the ocean at night. The killer waits for the right moment and follows the man outside, closing the glass door behind him

The musician stands at the end of the pier. Staring out over the railing and watching the waves breaking some twenty feet below. He takes a long, slow drag from his cigarette and inhales deeply. He seems deep in thought, perhaps reflecting on his evening performance in the bar. He is unaware that he is no longer alone. The killer steps closer to him, moving silently in the direction of the oblivious man while humming out loud the Elton John tune the musician seems to recognize.

The man turns at once and stares at the killer who is now just a few feet away. He squints as if trying to focus on the stranger before him. He glances at the glass doors as if wondering where this stranger appeared from…and why he hadn't heard him approaching. Standing face to face now the musician asks, "Were you at the show tonight?" The killer replies with merely a nod. With confusion and now a slight hint of concern, the musician continues…"Are you a fan of…" Suddenly, he feels the cold blade enter his chest…pain and terror grip him as he drops his cigarette. He opens his mouth to scream but only silent cries emerge from his lips as he is rendered helpless by the metal sticking out of him. The outside world begins to dim around him. He can no longer hear the crashing of the waves below or feel the warmth of the nighttime ocean breeze. He is suddenly grabbed by the shoulders and lifted off his feet. As he is being hurled over the railing the killer answers his question…"fear and death…only a fan of fear and death."

The killer inhales deeply to compose himself. He reaches into his pocket again. He pulls out his sunglasses and fits them over his eyes before opening the glass door to the mall. He lowers his head upon re-entering the crowded shopping area and heads briskly to the escalators. Retracing his steps past the clothing shops, he senses his pace is too rapid. He begins to worry that he may draw suspicion and silently scolds himself for his carelessness. He decides that the wiser course of action is to slow down and appear casual. He raises his head and begins to whistle a happy tune. He even pauses outside of a music store across from the food court. Pretending to window shop, he moves his eyes from an electric guitar with a small amplifier…then to a shiny red drum set. Something else catches his eye…not a something actually…but someone…a reflection in the store window coming from a table in the food court behind him…he recognizes the face and the stare…the man from the casino restroom.

4

Matthew Darden opens his eyelids, squinting as his brown eyes struggle to adjust to the morning light. Sitting up in bed, he stares at the window and watches the raindrops trail down the glass like tiny serpents. The damp, musty smell of the summer storm begins to fill the small apartment. He had been in the middle of a dream when a clap of thunder awakened him. The details of the dream are hazy and the images both confusing and disturbing…as most of his dreams are. He was riding on a Ferris Wheel…pleasant sounds of laughter and wonderful smells of funnel cakes and cotton candy filling the warm summer air. The little girl sitting next to him was wearing a pretty, yellow dress and was smiling with delight…the wind blowing through her long, blonde hair. They wave each time the wheel passes the ground, shouting and blowing kisses to a smiling woman staring up at them. He feels completely at peace, savoring each pleasing moment of the ride. Soon, an uneasiness comes upon him...a feeling of unimaginable despair. With each pass, he tries to focus on the woman standing below. His view of her always cloudy and blurry, as if she is surrounded in a dense fog. He tries to call out to her, warning her as if there is some horrible danger lurking nearby. His cries to her are muffled by the noise of the ride and the laughter of the little girl sitting next to him. With the pleasurable ride now becoming a nightmare, he pleads to the little girl next to him to listen. The young girl only responds with more laughter...as if she is unable to see or hear him...as if he is invisible. The giant wheel turns faster now, shaking as if it will become dislodged, hurling them both to a certain death. He reaches out to the little girl, trying to pull her nearer to him...trying to embrace her and protect her...Suddenly, the pretty girl's face is transformed into that of a woman. She continues to laugh hysterically...no longer a pleasant laugh of delight...but a maniacal, evil laugh. Just before he awakens, he sees the woman's face now covered in blood.

Matthew shakes his head forcefully as if trying to expel the unsettling imagery of the dream from his mind. A sadness comes over him…a recognition that he is so abnormal, and that his life is so empty. Deep in sorrow, his eyes begin to well with tears. He catches himself as he crosses his arms tightly around his own shoulders. Rocking back and forth, he repeats to himself "please don't leave me alone…please don't leave me here alone." He mutters this line continuously, although unsure of its meaning. For whatever reason, this is a ritual he repeats often in the moments of his darkest despair. It seems to bring him closer to something or someone…it seems to bring him peace. After several minutes, he settles himself enough to finally rise from the bed.

He walks slowly out of the bedroom and down the hallway to the kitchen. Reaching up into the cupboard, he grabs a glass and fills it with tap water. He furiously drinks the first glass to combat the feeling of dehydration that has settled over him. He quickly chugs down another before setting the glass into the sink and returning to the bedroom. Matthew grabs a pair of blue jeans and a blue Nike tee shirt from the floor. Slipping quickly into the wrinkled clothing, he turns around and faces the computer screen. He stares at the monitor, frozen in fear as he reads the words spelled out on the screen in capital letters.

"YOU ARE NOT ALONE...TIME IS RUNNING OUT!!"

Thousands of thoughts at once enter his mind. He has no recollection of typing these words himself and has no idea of the meaning behind the message...."YOU ARE NOT ALONE". A dreadful feeling comes over him that he is being watched...that at this minute he is in fact not alone. He begins a frantic search of the apartment...checking under the bed and peeking into closets. He searches the bathroom, ripping open the gray shower curtain...half expecting a horrible creature from his darkest nightmares to leap out and slash him with its fierce and bloody claws. The hairs on his neck and forearms stand at attention as he continues to scour the apartment...behind the couch in the living room and even the cabinets under the kitchen sink. His frenzied hunt produces nothing...no sign of anything or anyone in the apartment. He feels little relief as he is certain that he was not the author of the cryptic message. Matthew Darden's heart races as he gazes out of the bedroom window and plots his next move. He decides that what he must do is what he dreads the most…what he fears and avoids at all costs…he must leave the apartment and face the outside world…and whatever awaits him out there.

He grabs the keys off the nightstand and once again heads down the hallway. He reaches the front door, releases the deadbolt, and slowly turns the doorknob. Stepping cautiously outside of the apartment, he checks to the left and right, moving slowly and deliberately. Satisfied that he is safe to proceed, he inches his way along the narrow staircase. With the wood beneath the stained carpet creaking under his feet, he finds his way down the two flights of stairs and into the lobby. Matthew pauses at the three rows of mailboxes on the far wall. He finds his name and apartment number on one of the small, rectangular boxes…Matthew Darden – Apartment 207. He flips through the keys in his hand until he locates the small mailbox key and inserts it. Opening the box, he finds a single white envelope with the handwritten letters **M.**

Darden. Aside from the printed name on the envelope, the front is otherwise blank…no address and no postage. Matthew carefully opens the envelope and pulls out the eight neatly-folded twenty-dollar bills inside. He counts the money quickly and places the envelope in the pocket of his jeans and heads for the doors which lead outside.

Wildwood is still crowded, even in mid-August. Although the busiest part of the summer season is over and the early morning thunderstorm has delayed activity on the beaches, crowds still bustle along Atlantic Avenue. As Matthew stands in front of the Ocean Wind Apartments, he tries to acquaint himself once again with the outside world. He observes the commotion around him of a summer morning at the New Jersey Seashore. He begins the long walk down Atlantic Avenue as the hands of the big clock outside Shore Savings & Loan move past 11:00am. Along the way, he passes two surf shops, two arcades, and a beach bar. He sees a middle-aged woman with a straw hat pedaling a ten-speed bike, a family of four walking in order from biggest to smallest…beach clothes and towels in hand. He watches the cars passing by him, including a Mustang convertible driven by an attractive blonde in a bikini top and a pickup truck loaded with blonde surfer types…surfboards stacked in the truck bed. Matthew passes East Garfield Avenue, where he is nearly struck by a Frisbee thrown by a teenager. Finally, reaching the intersection of East Cedar Avenue, he turns right at the Sunset Café….the display clock in its parking lot now approaching 11:15am. East Cedar leads all the way to the boardwalk and famous Morey's Piers, a cluster of three amusement parks and two water parks sprawled out on three large oceanside piers.

As he arrives at the park, Matthew notices that the growing heat of the day hasn't discouraged crowds. Lines have formed at almost every ride and more visitors seem to arrive by the second. Matthew heads over to the wooden fence near the exit of the huge water slides. He entertains himself by observing the brave riders being hurled down yellow, plastic tubes and finally ejected into cold pools of heavily chlorinated water. He walks over to the roller coaster and stands mesmerized as he watches car after car of thrill seekers being buckled into their seats and launched through a series of loops and corkscrews, yelling and squealing with delight. Matthew stands and watches this activity until his legs grow tired. He also becomes aware of his growing hunger. He wonders over to the hot dog stand and purchases a foot long and coke with one of the twenty-dollar bills in his pocket. After accepting his change from a heavy-set balding man, he selects an empty table near the giant Ferris Wheel. Sitting alone at the table, his interest turns to a man and little girl sitting at the table next to him. The man is smiling at the child as she swirls her French Fries in a sea of ketchup. The little girl's face lights up when she spots a costumed character handing out balloons at the far end of the food court. She grabs the man's arm and leads him out of his seat and toward the balloons, leaving the remaining fries and mess of ketchup behind. Matthew's eyes continue to follow them. A sadness begins to take hold of him along with a faint recognition…a memory. He becomes increasingly aware that this event is in some way familiar, as if he has been here before…as if watching a rerun of some old production. Memories begin to form around him…familiar sights, sounds, and smells. He feels as if the details are right there within his reach…and yet so far. He focuses his mind, trying to grasp the hidden meaning behind it…if only he could remember. The image slowly fades, leaving

Matthew alone again…lost once again in his hopeless, forgotten world. He takes a final bite of the hot dog, a last swig of the cola…and moves on.

He stands at the entrance of the giant wheel and gazes up to the heavens. Holding one hand to shield the rays of the bright afternoon sun, he watches the huge wheel turn. Matthew notices the father and daughter from the food court have made their way through the long line, waiting their turn on the ride. They make their way hand in hand to one of the swinging cars, an attendant lowering the safety bar across their waists. Matthew watches them ascend to the top and descend back down again, the little girl holding up her arms in glee. His eyes stay locked on the pair as they pass by him again and again. As the car ascends for the fifth time, the girl mysteriously makes eye contact with Matthew, smiling and waving at him. Matthew returns her wave and smiles, although confused by her behavior. As the ride begins to slow, the girl's eyes continue to stare…not at Matthew any longer, but behind him. A look of concern appears on her young face as she seems to be pointing now to something which frightens her.

Matthew turns his head just in time to see a man shoving his way through the crowd and heading directly toward him. He doesn't recognize the dark-haired stranger who approaches him, but he immediately fears him. Matthew begins to run as fast as his legs will carry him, weaving his way around a maze of people, lamp posts and park benches. He darts through the amusement park, looking over his shoulder as the stranger follows close behind him. Matthew exits the park and continues to gallop up East Cedar Avenue, crossing the street this time and running through backyards toward Ocean Drive. He is nearly struck by a tan Lexus as he crosses the street...sounds of a horn blowing and the driver shouting behind him. He dares not stop...he senses that stopping will be the end of him...as if death itself is pursuing him. With his pulse racing and his chest heaving, he leaps over a picket fence and continues to dash through the backyards. He runs another hundred yards or so without looking back. Finally turning his head again to see that the man is no longer behind him, he crawls under the wooden porch of an old Victorian bed and breakfast.

Several minutes pass before he feels safe enough to crawl out from under the porch. Matthew briskly dusts himself off and moves to the side of the house. As he looks down Ocean Drive, he sees the man who was chasing him walking away in the distance. He is far enough away, but Matthew remains cautious. He slowly removes himself from the side of the house and carefully follows the stranger. He moves stealthily behind trees and parked cars, all the while keeping the man in his sights. The August afternoon sun bakes the pavement around him, creating heat waves rising from his feet as he walks. He follows the man for several more blocks down Ocean Drive and tails him as he turns onto East Baker…past an Elementary school and an old library. Finally taking cover behind the trunk of an elm tree, he watches as the man starts down the sidewalk of a small, yellow ranch house. Matthew is surprised to see, parked in the driveway, the same tan Lexus that had almost struck him earlier. The stranger reaches the front door of the house and enters, slamming the door behind him. Matthew doubles back and crosses the street several houses away. He decides that he is safer to approach the yellow house from the side instead of the front. With vigilance, he moves toward the house for a closer view…and an answer to the mystery.

Matthew is now at the side of the house,

standing on his tiptoes and trying to see inside the window. He carefully peers over the window pane, straining his eyes to focus. He is disappointed to discover that the glass has been covered from the inside by black plastic…possibly a garbage bag. He moves around the house to one of the front windows. This window is uncovered and allows him a view of what appears to be the living room. He can see that the room is mostly empty, and the house doesn't appear lived in. Only a single card table and two chairs are set up inside. On top of the table, he notices a pizza box and two open cans of Budweiser. He sees no sign of movement within the house. Pressing the side of his face against the glass, he tries to get a better view of the far side of the room. This side appears to be empty as well except for a mysterious black device sitting on the floor which resembles a tape recorder. Attached to the instrument is a wire with a wand-like microphone attached to the end of it. As he continues to study the strange object, something else catches his eye…something he hadn't previously noticed in the room. Behind the tape recorder, leaning against the wall…a black rifle with a scope attached. Knots form in Matthew's throat and stomach. He realizes that he is up against something more menacing than he had first imagined. His will has been broken. He suddenly realizes that he is unarmed and alone. Although disappointed in his himself for his lack of courage, he feels smaller now...helpless and vulnerable. He knows he must leave right now. He ducks down beneath the window and crawls back to the side of the house. After putting a safe distance between himself and the window, he stands and begins to run. He sprints back down East Cedar...then onto Ocean. He dashes past pedestrians who stare at him curiously...he darts past parked cars and mailboxes. He doesn't stop running until he is safely back on Atlantic Avenue and standing in front of the Ocean Wind Apartments.

Matthew hurries into the building and ascends the stairs two at a time to his apartment. With a trembling hand, he reaches into his pocket and finds the door key. All in one motion, he opens the door, slams it behind him and latches the deadbolt. He pulls a chair from the small dining room table and leans it against the front door. Finally allowing himself to catch his breath, he collapses on the living room floor, his back to the wall. Matthew brings his hands to his face, runs his hands through his hair...and begins to sob.

5

She steps through the large glass door and starts down the concrete steps of the courthouse. She carries a black leather bag and is dressed in a business suit with a black skirt and a neatly buttoned white blazer. She stops briefly to converse with a pair of male colleagues, smiling brightly as she greets them. Her every movement is blatantly flirtatious and seems to beg their attention. Fussing with her long blonde hair and, moving her hand slowly down her neckline as she speaks, she draws her male acquaintances' stares to her chest. She makes a point to initiate contact with them, touching them on the shoulder or squeezing an elbow as she continues the animated conversation.

She bends down and pretends to adjust the heel of her shoe, showing off her long, beautiful legs in the process. She appears to be in her mid-twenties and would be defined by most red-blooded males as an attractive woman…intelligent yet sexy. Her manner also conveys a certain assertiveness…a woman who knows what she wants and knows how to get it. Also, by definition…a manipulator.

As the killer stands in front of the newspaper kiosk across the street, pretending to be engrossed in an article about some sleazy local politician, he watches her and loathes the sight of her. To him, she is everything that is wrong in today's beauty-obsessed and shallow world. She is a woman of intelligence, certainly, but also a self-absorbed and heartless woman. A wealthy, spoiled diva who preys upon lonely and desperate men. He can assess this merely by the sight of her. He has seen her kind and he has dealt with them in the manner that they have treated others…harshly. As the young woman bids farewell to her male friends and starts her long walk down Park Boulevard, she is unaware that she has been studied…studied and chosen.

She waits for the streetlight to change and the green "walk" sign to illuminate. She crosses the street and heads directly in his direction now. He raises the newspaper higher, concealing his face from her view. The young woman stops briefly at the newsstand, now just a few feet from him. He can smell her perfume as she pulls a magazine off the rack. She quickly scans through the pages before replacing it and starting back down the sidewalk. He pauses, waiting until she is a safe distance away and begins to follow her. As he follows her steps down the sidewalk, he notices that the air has grown suddenly warm and damp. He sees dark clouds starting to form on the horizon ahead. He looks up at a display clock outside of an office building that now reads 5:11pm. The evening rush has begun. Workers have emerged from their small cubicles, where they have completed another day of staring at computer screens. Cars and buses flow past him in an endless tidal wave of chaos. She is now halfway up the boulevard, checking her watch occasionally as she continues her stroll. The route will take her past several buildings…past the bus terminal…past an Indian Restaurant…and finally, to the parking garage. He knows this route because, unbeknownst to her, he has made this journey with her…several times actually…following sometimes just a few paces behind her.

Today, he smiles as he walks behind her. He smiles because he is superior, not just to her, but to all others as well. He is also encouraged by the control he has developed over his talents. He still feels the occasional twinges in his forearm, tiny jolts of mild pain and itching like weak electric currents running through his veins. Although he is unable to fully understand how, he can talk himself back from the evil place where it wishes to drag him. He is becoming a more perfect machine. As he walks proudly among the other pedestrians on the sidewalk around him, the first drops of an afternoon rain begin to fall. The sudden appearance of the rain sends the crowd running for cover. The young woman he is following begins a slow jog also. She covers her head with her black bag as she runs, now just a block away from the parking garage. She turns off the sidewalk and scampers under the sign welcoming commuters to "Whitman's Park and Ride", a three-level indoor parking facility. She walks by a heavy-set male attendant standing in a small booth accepting cash from passengers waiting to exit. She smiles at him as she passes by, he returns her smile with a long stare…seemingly undressing the woman with his eyes. She reaches the elevators and pushes the button, waiting for the doors to open.

The killer waits around the corner by a cement wall, adjusting his clothing and pretending to be recovering from the soaking rain. He pauses until the doors part and the young blonde steps into the elevator. After a quick glance around the corner, he darts for the staircase and bolts up the stairs to the third floor. It is on this level where the young woman parks her car. Day after day, she arrives at the same time, 8:45am…too late for one of the more desirable lower-level spots. Finally reaching the third level, the killer throws open the door to find that she has emerged from the elevator and is walking in the direction of her car, a shiny, black BMW. He walks slowly and patiently behind her. She is still unaware of being followed, as she places her black leather bag on the floor of the garage near her vehicle. She leans over the bag, beginning to dig for her keys. As she is momentarily distracted, he reaches into the front pocket of his blue jeans, pulling out a brown piece of rope. As the young woman reaches her vehicle, the killer leaps quickly toward her. She turns and meets his wild eyes as a horrified scream emerges from her lips. He suddenly hears an unexpected sound above her screams…a car engine. He turns his head to see the vehicle accelerating quickly toward them.

He is unable to make out the features of the passengers and has no time to discern them. He pushes himself quickly from the woman and dives out of the way of the vehicle. The young woman falls to the floor as well, covering her head with her hands and screaming as the car narrowly misses her. Just before impact with her black BMW, the car's brakes lock. As the vehicle screeches to a sudden stop, the killer can get a better look at the color and make…a tan Lexus. The driver leaps out of the tan car and begins running toward him , holding a pistol in his right hand. The killer is somehow able to lift himself from the cold garage floor and begins to flee. He keeps his body low, crouching behind parked cars and vehicles as he moves. The stranger with the gun seems to lose sight of him now, pointing the weapon in one direction, then another. The killer crouches behind a parked Volkswagen Jetta, feverishly plotting his next move. The man in the passenger's seat of the tan Lexus has now climbed out of the vehicle. He stands on the hood of a blue Honda Accord, scanning his eyes over the parking garage. The stranger with the pistol retracts his weapon, placing it back in his coat pocket. Other vehicle owners are starting to crowd around now, witnessing the curious spectacle. The stranger with the gun motions the other man toward him. Without hesitation, the two strangers quickly bolt for the staircase, leaving the killer still crouched behind the Volkswagen but cornered.

His thoughts move rapidly from confusion…to anger…to desperation. He can now hear the reaction of those around him beginning to stir. He hears the young woman's cry for help…he hears a man shout an order for someone to call 911. He seems to be witnessing everything in slow motion now. He is too stunned to move and has not yet formulated a plan. He knows that very soon police will be summoned, witnesses will be questioned, and a manhunt will begin for him. He knows beyond the shadow of a doubt that he must act now…and act quickly. He recalls the saying…the doctrine…that true beauty lies on the other side of fear. He rises from his crouched position…quickly and decisively. He moves toward the stunned crowd, who merely stand watching him, frozen in silence. He runs to the tan Lexus, its engine still running and in the same position it's been since being brought to an abrupt halt moments earlier. He dives into the vehicle and throws the gear shift into reverse. The vehicle lurches backward, striking the rear end of a white Ford Taurus in the process. Ignoring the sounds of the metal on metal impact, he moves the gear shift into drive and spins the vehicle around, starting down the ramp toward the lower levels of the parking garage.

He lays on the horn and swerves around a slow-moving pickup truck…he nearly runs over an elderly woman carrying a potted plant, sending her diving to the ground for cover and the plant flying. The vehicle reaches the lower level of the garage. He can now see the eyes of the heavy-set parking attendant growing wider at the sight of the accelerating vehicle rapidly approaching. The killer sees that three other cars are lined up at the parking garage exit. He swerves into the unused second exit lane, pushes the accelerator to the floor, and crashes through the wooden arm, splintering it in two. One of the pieces bounces off the hood of the Lexus and smashes into the windshield, causing the glass to crack like ice on a frozen pond. The vehicle falls forward as it exits the parking garage. Seemingly airborne for a brief second, the car smashes down on the pavement of Park Boulevard. The killer slams on the brakes with all his might, causing the tires to lock up with an ear-piercing squeal. Cars on either side of him also come to a sudden stop, one of them just missing the passenger side door of the Lexus. He pulls the steering wheel to the left, leaving a trail of rubber on the pavement as he launches the vehicle forward again. His heart is racing as he checks the rear-view mirror, then the road ahead of him. Relieved to see no sign of police or the two unwelcomed visitors from the parking garage, he abruptly turns the vehicle off Park Boulevard…onto Lincoln Drive…then onto Industrial Drive. He jerks the wheel again, turning into the parking lot of a warehouse that appears to be abandoned. He drives around the back of the building and stops near some old railroad tracks. Sweating profusely, he jogs down the tracks. Only when he is satisfied that he is a safe distance from the incriminating Lexus does he stop running. The killer climbs a small hill, walks into a densely-wooded area, and collapses from exhaustion.

6

The tram car lumbers along the Wildwood Boardwalk, chugging past arcades, ice cream stands, and t-shirt shops. The trams are a familiar sight along the Jersey Shore and are famous for both their appearance, bright yellow, and the repetitive voice coming from the speakers of the cars themselves. The recorded voice is female, and every couple of minutes warns pedestrians to "watch the tram car please". The locals know that the voice on the recording belongs to Floss Stingel, the girlfriend of the original owner of the tram company. She recorded the phrase in 1971, and it has become synonymous with the city. The phrase is even printed on bumper stickers and t-shirts sold in the shops along the boardwalk. A trip to Wildwood is not complete without a tram ride.

This afternoon, Matthew Darden is seated in the rear of one of the trams. Lately, he has enjoyed riding on the small electric cars, and sometimes spends hours traveling up and down the three mile stretch of the boardwalk. He has spent many an afternoon observing the tourists getting on and off the cars…some of them neatly dressed for lunch or shopping, others covered in sand and smelling of sunscreen. He always sits quietly and watches, rarely speaking a word to anyone. The ride offers him a feeling of peace…as if he is merely a spectator watching a performance…a feeling that nothing is expected from him. He is just another passenger…just like the rest of them.

Today's ride is a particularly welcomed one. Matthew has spent the morning walking aimlessly. His legs are tired, and he is somewhat agitated. He found himself wandering around the amusement park again. Once more he stood staring at the roller coaster and water slides. He stopped and stared at the giant Ferris Wheel for over half an hour. He has repeated this ritual several times before, on many recent summer days like this one. Today seems different in some way. Today, he feels as if he is making one final visit to this place. As if winds of change are blowing…an unseen storm brewing on the horizon. An undeniable feeling washing over him…a realization that his life is about to be forever altered. He can't comprehend why he feels this way, but despite any attempt to try to push this feeling into the back of his mind, he cannot. Although memories, even short-term ones, usually elude him…this one is etched deeply in his mind. A clear recollection of that yellow house…the tan Lexus in the driveway…the shotgun. He knows beyond the shadow of a doubt that he is at a crossroads. Matthew knows that he must do the unthinkable…he must face his fear and return to that yellow house. Despite the danger and the terror of the unknown, he must act. He is sure the house is hiding a secret…he is drawn to it…he needs to know.

The afternoon is slowly making its way toward dusk when Matthew arrives at the yellow house. The sun begins to move low in the sky to the west as he stands behind the old elm tree across the street. The heat of the day has now given way to cooler temperatures, and a slight breeze gently shakes the tree limbs. As he gazes at the house, Matthew notices that the tan Lexus is now absent from the driveway. The thought occurs to him that the absence of the car may indicate that the two strangers have moved on...or at least are gone for now. The former would be a much bigger relief to Matthew than the latter. At any rate, he knows that now is his chance to get a closer look. He tells himself that he must overcome his fear and press on. Pleading with his feet to move despite his growing anxiety, he pulls himself away from the elm tree and quickly crosses the street...crouching low as he moves to the side of the house. He ducks under the bushes of the neighboring house and scans the property around him, searching for any sign of movement. For the moment, all is quiet, the evening breeze the only noise around him. He begins to rise from the bushes and start for the yellow house when he hears a vehicle pull onto the street, heading in his direction. He dives quickly back into the bushes, looking up to discover that the incoming vehicle is not a tan Lexus, but a white van.

The van slows briefly in front of the house, then continues down the street. Just to be safe, Matthew waits until the van is completely out of view before emerging from the bushes. He starts once again toward the house. He ducks past the side window, which is still covered by the black plastic material. On all fours now, he crawls to the window on the other side of the house. He stands, stretching to get a glance inside. The table and chairs are still there, but the pizza box and beer cans are gone. Also absent from the room is the strange-looking recording device, as well as the shotgun. Matthew begins to convince himself that the two strangers are indeed gone as well. He breathes a sigh of relief and turns from the window to leave…suddenly wanting to end this day and return to the safety of his apartment. He turns just in time to see the white van return, slowing in front of the house. This time the van comes to a complete stop. A man leaps out of its sliding side door…he yells in Matthew's direction, "STAY RIGHT WHERE YOU ARE!!!"

For a brief second, Matthew stands frozen in stunned silence. His brain begs his feet to move, but he is temporarily paralyzed with fear. "I SAID STAY RIGHT THERE!!!", the man yells again.

Staring at him, Matthew vaguely recognizes this man, though he doesn't seem to be the person who had chased him before. The man is less than fifty feet from him now and closing quickly. As Matthew turns and begins to flee toward the back of the house, something else begins to disturb him. It is so subtle at first that he's able to distract himself, but very soon it begins to consume him. He is unable to move now, but it is also impossible to stay still. This is unlike any panic attack he has experienced before...this is something entirely different. First, on the underside of his forearm, radiating to the base of his hand...an itching. He begins to sweat uncontrollably, his breath now coming in short pants. It's as if an army of ants have burrowed into his skin, tunneling deeper into him. He imagines his insides are ablaze and he will soon explode into dust. He is no longer concerned about the men who pursue him or what kind of harm they wish upon him. At this moment, death would be a welcomed relief...he just wants the misery to go away. "MAKE IT STOP!!!...MAKE IT STOP!!" He collapses to the ground, so consumed with the horror of it all...he barely notices the man who was chasing him standing over him now. The man stares down at him, a long syringe in his hand.

As Matthew Darden drifts into blackness, he hears only a final gust of evening breeze…and the man saying, "close your eyes, just close your eyes now."

7

He dreams of the amusement park and the giant wheel. He is the lone passenger on the ride. Glittering reflections of neon surround him. As he passes the ground each time, he sees two dark figures. They grab at him, attempting to pull him off the ride. He feels their fingers around him, scratching him. Their faces and bodies are transformed now, they have become two hideous looking creatures…monsters with slimy hands reaching out for him. In the distance, he hears the giggles of a little girl and the voice of a woman…calling out to him. Shrouded in darkness, he is unable to see their faces. The men are laughing at him …mocking him. The scene changes to the car crash now…upside down…trails of raindrops and blood running down his cheeks…the hum of the motor…the sound of approaching sirens. He hears a man talking to him now. At first, his voice is an unrecognizable mumble, and his face a blur. The man is trying to tell him something. As Matthew focuses intently on the person standing over him, he realizes that he is no longer dreaming…he is wide awake, in pain, and frightened.

He is strapped to what looks like a hospital bed and is lying on a cold, gray mattress. As he squints his eyes to adjust to the bright light over his head, he quickly scans the room. The room resembles a basement, with exposed pipes running along one of the walls. He realizes that the water he heard in his dream were the dripping pipes, reminiscent of raindrops. As he turns his head again, he is overcome with pain…a sharp, burning pain deep in his right forearm. He is helpless to move, his arms tied securely to the posts of the bed. He cries out now, pleading loudly for help. Matthew hears footsteps moving toward him. Once again, the man stands over him…the same man who had chased him through the woods. He can see him more clearly now, a man who appears to be in his mid to late forties. The stranger has a husky build, dark hair, and is dressed in a plain, black sweater with a white encrusted logo on the chest. He wears dark, black dress pants and holds in his hand a thin, yellow manila folder. Before Matthew can utter another word, the man begins talking to him. "Listen to me and don't speak" the man tells him. "I'm aware that you are confused, scared, and in a lot of pain. I'm also very sorry about the restraints, but I assure you they are necessary. I am about to tell you some information. It is unlike anything you have heard before. The information I am going to tell you will help you understand your life, but it will not save it. It will not save you because you are already dead."

As Matthew opens his mouth to speak, he is silenced again by the stranger. "I promise that you will have a chance to speak, but first I need you to listen...I need you to listen and to help me." With that, the stranger opens the yellow folder in his hand and pulls out two photographs. He holds the first photo in front of Matthew. "Do you recognize the man in this picture?" Matthew squints his eyes again, focusing on the picture. The man in the photograph is handsome and well dressed. He appears to be in his forties, with a dark complexion and dark-brown eyes. The man is smiling and posing with a thumbs-up sign. He wears a look of confidence and accomplishment...the look of someone of importance. As Matthew stares intently at the photo, the man continues to speak. "Please concentrate, I need to know for sure...do you recognize this man?" After another moment of studying the photograph, Matthew shakes his head no. The man raises his voice now, shouting at Matthew..."THINK HARD, I NEED YOUR HELP!" Finally, Matthew can take no more. He shouts back at the man...causing him to drop the photograph..."NO, I'VE NEVER SEEN HIM BEFORE!...WHAT THE HELL IS THIS?...WHAT IS THIS ALL ABOUT?"

The man pauses and exhales loudly before picking the photograph from the floor and continuing. "The man in the picture is Thomas Van Allen, a highly successful executive in the automotive industry from Piscataway, New Jersey. Aside from his well-known business accomplishments, Mr. Van Allen has been linked to everything from gambling and extortion to arms dealing. He has also been linked to a terrorist group operating in the United States." The man pauses again, studying Matthew's reaction before continuing. "Approximately two months ago, Mr. Van Allen was killed by a single round to the head from a revolver outside the Quick Stop Convenience Store near the Garden State Parkway. He was found minutes later lying next to his black SUV in a pool of blood." A moment of silence passes before Matthew asks, "What does this have to do with me?" The man continues, "I will get to that after I show you one more picture...Do you recognize this man's face?" As Matthew again shakes his head no, the man begins his next dissertation. " The man in this photograph is Rico Satori, a fairly well-known piano player in Atlantic City. About two weeks ago, he went missing after playing a show in a casino bar. Four days later, his body washed up on the beach. An autopsy confirmed that he was most likely dead before he entered the water. The official cause of death was a knife wound to the chest. The blade was still sticking out of him when his body washed up. It is believed that, after he had finished his nightly show in the casino bar, he was followed. Police interviewed witnesses who said they had seen him nearby in the Pier Shops. Mall surveillance video also caught a picture of the man believed to be the killer. Witnesses also confirmed that the same man was in the casino earlier that evening. The photographs were turned over to federal agents. After successfully matching the photo with a suspect using their database...that's when we came in."

"Who are you?...and what does this have to do with me?" asks Matthew. The man continues..."I will get to that soon. Let's just say that we have access to information others do not and we know things no one else knows. We were able to match the photograph from the surveillance picture to the suspect. His name, as it turns out, is Patrick Hartley. The feds were not to match him using any of their data-bases but we were. The reason that the feds were not able to match him is because Patrick Hartley no longer exists. You see, Patrick Hartley died about three years ago. Now, I'm going to show you another photograph." The man reaches into the yellow folder for a final time. As Matthew stares at this photo, his eyes widen...his body begins to shake uncontrollably, and everything begins to move in slow motion. The man smiles knowingly and says..."Do you recognize *your* face, Patrick Hartley?"

8

His face is ghostly white, his heads is spinning, and his world has been turned upside down. He wants so badly not to believe. He wants to shout at the man to stop the lies. He wants his hands untied so that he can cover his ears with them and shout…"LEAVE ME ALONE!!." He wants to believe that he is in the middle of a bad nightmare and will wake up soon. He yearns to be back on the boardwalk, back on the tram car…his favorite place in the world. A place where he is normal and safe…a place where the sun always shines, and his shadow never falls. He seeks denial and a different reality, even though he knows the horrible truth. Somewhere deep in his soul, buried in a place he has chosen to forget…he knows the truth. He is not the helpless victim of circumstance…he is the monster from his dreams…he is the unseen evil that lurked in his apartment…he is the hidden menace that always seemed to follow him. While in the past, he had hoped to find meaning and an understanding to his life…now the only thought that brings him comfort is his death. He closes his eyes tightly now, praying for sleep to come…hoping his dreams will transport him to some other place…to anywhere but here. Before he can fall asleep, the man standing over him speaks again. "Stay with me Hartley…I need you to stay with me now. There is much more I need to tell you…there is much more that you need to hear."

"First of all," the man continues, "the pain in your arm should be starting to subside now. You have been given an anesthetic for discomfort and the INR Unit has been removed. I will explain to you what that means, but first let me explain who I am. My name is Dr. Stadnik. My partner, who you will meet later, is Dr. Benjamin Felton. Up until very recently, you were part of a project…a project initiated by our own government. Mr. Hartley, the United States has been at war since September 11, 2001. The people we are fighting are completely committed to their cause…this is what makes them so dangerous…the fact that they are willing to die for their cause. Because of this, the United States' Government adopted a policy known as "No Holds Barred" The purpose of this policy was to explore ways, whatever means necessary, to deal with the threat. Under this policy, we have been able to thwart many attacks before they happened. Unfortunately, when we find one way to deal with these terrorists, they find another way. They are always one step ahead. It's only a matter of time before they carry out another successful attack, and we believe the next one will be far worse than anything we have ever seen before." Patrick Hartley, as he is now being called, has been lying there listening to Dr. Stadnik for what seems like an eternity without interrupting. He wants to understand but none of this is making any sense to him. "What does any of this have to do with me?", Patrick asks. Dr. Stadnik takes a deep breath and sighs before continuing.

"Several years ago, a self-funded scientist from Missouri began working on a project. This project involved a theory known as INR or Induced Nerve Response. His research was impressive although controversial. Eventually it was funded by our government under "No Holds Barred." My partner, Dr. Felton, spearheaded the project along with this other scientist. The theory was that a subject fitting a certain profile could be "implanted" with an artificial response mechanism…basically a small device planted inside the body. This small device could then act as a sort of driver of programmed nerve response. In order to visualize this properly Mr. Hartley, think of a remote car starter. At the appropriate time, with a press of the button, the engine starts. Similarly, in this case, the subject is programmed to respond to a certain action. That action is then carried out at the appropriate time. It's much more technical than that, but that is basically it in layman's terms. As you may have surmised by now, Mr. Hartley, you were among the subjects. You were the first official subject as a matter of fact. I say first official subject, because the concept itself is not new. In fact, it has long been suspected that INR has been used before. As early as 2008, a commercial airliner crashed near the Russian town of Omsk, killing all 158 passengers on board. When the accident was investigated, no weather-related problems were found in the area near the time of crash. Also, they found no evidence of engine or rudder malfunction. What they did find was even more alarming. It seems the pilot drove the plane straight into the ground. This was a pilot with an otherwise spotless record and thousands of hours of flying time. The incident was officially declared pilot error, but we all suspected something more. When the cockpit recorder was discovered, these suspicions increased. On those tapes, the pilot is heard arguing with the co-pilot and first officer seconds before impact. The voice on the recording is clearly the pilot's but he sounded like a different man...a madman." Hartley starts to speak again but is immediately cut off by Stadnik. "Let me finish and then you can speak... In 2012, a subway crash in London killed dozens of commuters when the train jumped the track and slammed directly into a concrete wall. When the scene was investigated, it was discovered that the train's throttle was still in the forward-most position. In other words, the driver had essentially launched the train directly into the wall. Once again, Mr. Hartley, the incident was ruled an error. After hearing witness accounts of the driver's behavior just before the accident, we discovered some very disturbing similarities between these two instances. These are just two examples. There was also a case of a seemingly normal woman who woke up one day and strolled into a Texas hospital with a handgun. There have also been cases of assassination attempts on leaders around the world by individuals who fit the profile. The individuals who committed these acts all seem to have one thing in common, a history or TBI...Traumatic Brain Injury. This is the one essential ingredient to make a person a candidate for manipulation. Are you beginning to understand what we are up against here?'

Patrick Hartley lies on the bed in stunned silence. There are countless questions racing through his mind as he struggles to absorb this blizzard of information. He can think of only one question to ask..."Why me?...Why would you choose me?" Dr. Stadnik hesitates before replying, a look of shame now appearing on his face. "Actually, that is a great question. Do you recall when I mentioned earlier that a subject must fit a certain profile...you fit that profile, Mr. Hartley. You fit the profile because of your condition. Allow me to circle back for a moment. Approximately three years ago, you were involved in a tragic car accident along the Atlantic City Expressway. By the time you were pulled from the wreckage, you had slipped into a deep coma. You remained in that state for a period of almost eight months. During that time, various tests were carried out to determine the extent of the damage to your brain. The determination was made that you had suffered irreversible brain damage. Even if there was any hope you would awaken, you would have no memory and very limited motor function. Since you had no family members for doctors to consult, it was only a matter of time before the hospital would petition the state to terminate life support. This is when we stepped in. You see, Mr. Hartley, the accident took your life from you...it took your mind from you as well. This made you the perfect subject, an open and blank canvas so to speak. A relatively youthful man with no family, no friends that anyone knew of. So that was the day Patrick Hartley died...and Matthew Darden was born."

A fury of anger begins to overtake him now. He begins to thrash in the bed, moving his arms back and forth furiously in effort to break the straps that bind him. His rage is transformed into a verbal tirade as he begins screaming at the top of his lungs. "YOU SELFISH BASTARDS!!...YOU STOLE MY LIFE!!!...YOU SON OF A

BITCH!!!...I'LL KILL YOU...YOU UNDERSTAND ME!!!...I WILL KILL YOU!!!" Dr. Stadnik maintains his calm as he stares back. "Mr. Hartley", he begins, "all the anger in the world will not help you now. What is done is done. We must only deal with the present. I need your help. I am your only hope, Mr. Hartley, and you are mine." Something in what Stadnik said..."I am your only hope...and you are mine." He recalls hearing those words somewhere before...but where?...when? Suddenly, he begins to recall the reoccurring dream. As if he is back there again...the dream of lying in the car...the smell of blood and gasoline...a man standing over him, a dark figure...that man also spoke those words to him. " It was you, wasn't it?" Hartley asks. "It was you that night...the accident...you were there weren't you?" Dr. Stadnik begins to nod slowly. As Hartley studies his face, he notices again the look on the man's face...a look of regret...a look of shame. " Yes, I was there that night, Mr. Hartley."

"As you can see, your memory is beginning to return to you. With the removal of the INR Unit, more memories will return over time. I need to warn you, Mr. Hartley, some of what you recall will terrify you...worse than any nightmare you can imagine. The time has come for you to know, for us to help each other. I need to make you understand. I must tell you more about the founder of this research. You need to remain calm and you need to listen. So many lives depend on you, Mr. Hartley, starting with your own. As I told you before, he was a little-known scientist from Missouri. His name is Dr. Owen Darden. His last name should sound very familiar to you, Mr. Hartley. The few that were aware of his existence regarded his work as controversial, at best. All of that changed when news broke through the scientific community of his work with Induced Nerve Respond. The pressure on our government to seize control of this technology was enormous. I'm sure you can appreciate the ramifications of his findings ending up in the wrong hands. Dr. Darden's project was secretly funded with him in full control. From there, work was quickly underway, developing the technology and finding an ideal subject. The project was given a name…The Darden Pursuit. As you now know, Mr. Hartley, you were that first subject. Once the INR device was implanted, you assumed a programmed identity known as Matthew001. The first name was chosen after Dr. Darden's first-born son who was the victim of an unsolved murder some years ago. This is how you came to know yourself as Matthew Darden. Because the project was so new, and many on the inside were skeptical of Dr. Darden, you were kept under constant surveillance. The skepticism of the others would soon prove to be valid. Dr. Darden suddenly vanished, and we lost track of our subject…I mean, we lost track of you. We now know that we have failed in the worst possible way. Dr. Darden is not who we thought he was. We now know, Mr. Hartley, that we have unleashed a madman. He is out there somewhere right now. You were the first subject, but you are not the last. There are more out there…more just like you…we don't know how many or what they are prepared to do. We only know that they are out there, and time is running out.

Patrick Hartley feels as if he has entered a dream-like state. He no longer feels as though he is awake. The words of this man, Dr. Stadnik, seem to float through the air and hang there…suspended. As he lies on the table, he no longer feels part of his own body. He feels like an empty-soul, a tiny feather being blown about in a breeze. In the last several minutes, his emotions have moved from disbelief…to anger…to hopelessness. He can no longer just lay here and listen. "I don't know what you want from me!!...you say you want my help?...I'm no one...and if what you are saying is true...why the hell would I help you?...I can't listen to this anymore...If you want to kill me then kill me!!!...Come on you bastard!!..you said it yourself...I'm already dead!...you want to tie me up and make me listen to lies?...make me crazier than I already am?...I can't help you...LEAVE ME ALONE!!" Again, Stadnik only stares. He lets him finish his tirade without interrupting. Only when he is sure that Hartley has finished does he continue. "You can help us, Mr. Hartley, you can help us and I'm betting you will...not for us...but for your wife and daughter."

A long moment of silence passes as the two men stare at each other...each waiting for the other to speak. Finally, it is Hartley who breaks the silence. "But you said...you said I have no family", his voice trembling along with the rest of his body. "No", Stadnik replies, "I said that's what **they** said...that's not what **I** said. You see, Mr. Hartley, you were not the only one in the car that night. But then again, you already knew that didn't you? Now, if we have an understanding, can I free your hands? There is something else I need to show you…something that will help you understand. Do I have your cooperation, Mr. Hartley?" After a brief pause, Hartley slowly nods his head yes. Stadnik releases him from the straps and leads him over to a small work desk in the far corner of the room. As Hartley begins to walk, slowly regaining the feeling in his legs, he finds that he is still very weak. He also becomes aware of a persistent throbbing emanating from the covered wound on his forearm. Stadnik notices his unsteadiness and pulls the chair out from under the work desk, motioning for him to sit. As he sits down, Hartley notices that there is a newspaper spread out on the desk, opened to page three. Stadnik points to the title of the article which reads **Accident Injures Four on A.C. Expressway**. "Read it, Mr. Hartley." Hartley begins to scan the article…

A thirty-three-year -old man traveling with his wife and three-year-old daughter was critically injured Saturday evening on the Atlantic City Expressway. Their car was struck head-on by another vehicle driven by an unidentified male. The critically-injured man was transported to a local hospital where he is being treated for severe head trauma and multiple lacerations. According

to reports, the victim, identified as Patrick Hartley of Wildwood, New Jersey, lost control of the vehicle and slid into on-coming traffic. Also, among the injured were his wife Kimberly, 34 and daughter Sarah Hartley, 3. Mother and daughter were treated for minor injuries and later released.

"I'm sure this is hard for you, Mr. Hartley. I know how badly you want to remember. I promise you, it will come back to you in time. In the meantime, we need to deal with the present. "What has happened in the past cannot be altered. I need you to focus on the here and now. There is more you need to know. Are you willing to listen to what I have to say?"

As Hartley turns to look at Stadnik, his vision is blurred. His eyes are filled with tears and he bites down hard on his lip to keep from sobbing. He wants to lash out…he wants to rise from the chair and punch a hole right through the man. He wants revenge for what they have done to him…for all the pain that they have caused. He wants the man to feel the pain that he feels…to understand the torture that is the unknown. There is only one fact that prevents him from seeking violent retribution. What if this man is telling the truth?

"As you can plainly see from the article, Mr. Hartley, your wife and daughter did survive. Their whereabouts are unknown, but some information did surface recently. We now have reason to believe that your wife has contacted another person, a female. She has apparently sought help and may have given information to her. We believe that she sought this woman's help specifically because of her occupation. We think that the woman she has confided in is Anna Holloway, some young attorney from Philadelphia. Whatever information your wife told this attorney has put them both in grave danger. Several days ago, Anna Holloway was attacked in a parking garage in broad daylight. Ms. Holloway did survive the attack and local police have investigated the incident as a simple robbery attempt. Obviously, because of the new information that has surfaced, we have reason to believe otherwise. Our belief is that the attack was the work of either Owen Darden himself or one of his men. We feel that this woman knows something…and Darden knows this. If Anna Holloway is indeed a target, Darden will come after her again. This may be our shot at him…this may be your only chance also. Simply put, find Anna Holloway before Darden gets to her and you may find your family. Do you understand now, Mr. Hartley? Once again, I am your only hope, and you are mine."

9

Anna Holloway walks quickly down Park Boulevard, keeping her head down and avoiding eye contact with other pedestrians as she passes the familiar bus terminal and Indian Restaurant. The city street is crowded during lunchtime and a small line is already forming outside the restaurant. The afternoon sky is a clear blue as she walks into a slight breeze that blows through her long, blonde hair. The late-summer day is nearly perfect, sunny and without a hint of rain. Within the breeze, she can detect a smattering of fall-chill to the air. She welcomes the cooler weather that is soon to come. She has always preferred autumn to summer. The cooler temperatures always remind her of cozy times with family and carefree afternoons back home in King of Prussia, PA. Autumn makes her think of her mother's delicious apple pies and, most of all, reminds her of her father. He was a tough but caring dad, hard-working and strong. She can almost still hear him, sitting in his favorite chair in the living room, watching his beloved Philadelphia Eagles on a Sunday afternoon. "Come on O-line, start blocking!!!...Come on offense, we need to score here!!" Her mother yelling from the kitchen..."Relax Frank, it's just a game." But football wasn't just a game to her father, it was a passion. That same passion he instilled in his daughter. Work hard for what you want...never quit. He was a carpenter and the son of a coal miner. Everyone in the town knew him and everyone seemed to love him. He worked so many long hours, saving enough money so that his daughter could attend college and have opportunities he never had. He encouraged her constantly, always believed in her. Eventually, Anna would work her way through university, then eventually through law school at Penn Law. She owes so much to her father, if only he could have hung on a little longer. He would have been so proud seeing her with that cap and gown, seeing her join the firm and become a practicing lawyer. Unfortunately, life doesn't always work out that way. He would pass away three days before her eighteenth birthday, God rest his soul. How she wishes he could be part of her life now. His guidance and reassurance would see her through the most difficult days. Fortunately, she still has her mother to guide her. Her mom Beverly, such a courageous woman. Even in the most trying time of her life, the death of her husband, her faith was never shaken. She carried on with courage and grace. How wonderful mothers are, she thinks to herself. Will she have the strength to a good mother? Will she have the courage to guide and lead by example?

While lost in thought, she realizes that she has now wandered past Whitman's Park and Ride. She is thankful that she wasn't paying attention when she passed it. Ever since that day and what happened to her…what nearly happened to her. "Stop it", she whispers to herself. She must remind herself not to let her mind drift back there again. It is a scary world and the city is a dangerous place. Random acts of violence happen almost daily here. In her career as a lawyer, she hears about things like this almost every day. She tells her mother, who worries about her constantly, this very thing. It would be more comforting, though, if she believed it herself. Despite her best efforts, a cold fear begins to take hold of her. Anna stops walking long enough to pause and catch her breath.

After a few more deep breaths, she is feeling much better. She lifts her head to take in her surroundings. She realizes that she has been standing in the same place for several minutes, lost in her thoughts. She takes note of a man standing next to her on the sidewalk, reading a newspaper…pretending to read a newspaper. She is aware that the man is spending more time sneaking looks at her, his eyes moving up and down her body. This is something she has become accustomed to, although it still makes her uneasy. Ever since Anna was a young girl, she has been aware of her physical beauty and has been reminded of it often. It is not something she boasts about, nor is it something that makes her feel somehow superior to others. It is instead, merely a fact. Beauty, after all, is not something that she has strived for or studied long hours in a library to achieve. It is something that was given to her…a gift from her parents. She is more appreciative of the things she has been able to achieve in adulthood. The many sacrifices she has made, the long hours of studying while friends were out partying and chasing boys. In truth, her physical appearance has helped her along the way. She is aware that her beauty allows her to stand out in a crowd. In the ultra-competitive world she lives in, any advantage is a bonus. As a young female attorney, it feels like every day is a struggle…a struggle to prove her herself…a struggle to defy the odds and succeed. Her competitive nature she also credits to her parents, particularly her father. Without these traits, she realizes, she would not be where she is today. Nothing and no one, Anna tells herself, will ever take that away from her. She is much too strong, and she has come too far. She has given herself these little pep talks countless times recently, ever since that afternoon in the parking garage. Despite her mother's worry and despite her own fears, she will not let one act of violence break her. She allows herself one more deep breath before pressing on.

She notices that the leering stranger with the newspaper has moved on now, as she continues to walk in the direction of the black BMW parked further down the street on Park Avenue. Recently, she has been parking in the extended lot a few block away. Today, because she only intended to put in a half-day of paperwork, she instead decided to take her chances on one of the metered spots on a side street. As she arrives at her vehicle, she is pleasantly surprised to see no parking ticket on her windshield. After unlocking the door and sliding into the shiny black sports car, Anna remembers the phone call she needs to make. She reaches into her designer black handbag and removes her cell phone, searching the contact list until she comes across the listing for "**MOM**". After three rings, the older woman's voice answers, "Is that you Anna?" Anna doesn't like to consider her mother old. If she is being truthful with herself, this is probably because of the death of her father. Admitting her mother is old scares her. Losing her father was devastating to Anna. The thought of losing both of her parents…unthinkable. "It's me, mom, can you make sure she is ready? I cut out early today and I'm coming to pick her up." She hears the little girl singing in the background as her mother answers, "she is ready and waiting for you. See you in a few minutes." Anna hangs up the phone and reaches for the radio dial, searching until she settles on a song…one of her favorites from Maroon 5. She starts to hum along, tapping her steering wheel to the beat of the music.

As she pulls out of the parking spot and starts up Park Boulevard, she is lost in thoughts of the beautiful little girl and the happy times to come. "Everything is going to be perfect" she tells herself. She is so deep in thought that she is unable to comprehend the loud popping noise…the crash of exploding glass from the drivers-side window. As her mind tries to quickly process what is happening, she feels the searing pain in the left side of her skull. Anna's last thought is the smiling face of a small angel…and her last words, "I'm so sorry little one…"

10

The skill of driving has returned surprisingly easily to Patrick Hartley, considering the many years it has been since he operated a vehicle. Although he doesn't remember ever driving, he seems to have the ability to do so. It is such a strange feeling to him when he does something purely out of instinct. It's like a Déjà vu moment, as if he has been somewhere and done something before, but just can't put his finger on when or why. That's what life has been like for him and, up until hours ago, he thought that's the way his life would be forever. However, as he moves the dark-green Toyota Camry steadily down the Pennsylvania Turnpike, a strange sense of calmness settles over him, along with a renewed sense of purpose. Amazingly, the pain in his arm has almost completed subsided. As he glances down quickly to look at the wound, he also notices that it seems to be no larger than a pin-prick. He is relieved that the physical pain is almost gone, even though mentally he is exhausted, and he finds himself still trying to process it all. He reminds himself that he must focus on his next destination.

Since his encounter with the mysterious Dr. Stadnik, and the knowledge that there may after all be some meaning to his life, a feeling of urgency has come over him. Merely the chance that his family may still be out there somewhere, however small that chance may be, has given him a renewed desire to press on. Perhaps the dense fog of hopelessness that seemed would surround him for eternity may be lifting. Maybe he has a reason to live…a chance to reclaim what has been so cruelly taken from him…a family…a precious daughter, and the love of a woman. Somewhere in the dark recesses of his mind, hidden behind shadow and dark despair, he always held tightly to hope. This feeling would often confuse him as he would pass through countless, meaningless days alone. He would often wonder to himself why he still felt any glimmer of optimism. Now, finally, on this day driving in the car given to him by the very man who helped put him in this position…he has a mission…and he has reason to hope.

As he continues his trip down the expressway, Patrick reaches over to the passenger seat and picks up the white envelope handed to him by Stadnik just before they parted ways. The inside of the envelope contains cash, five-thousand dollars according to Stadnik. Patrick didn't count the money before leaving, but he can only go on faith…what else does he have? Stadnik also handed him a business card before he left from the law firm of Garrity, Allen, and Cole. The person's name on the card is Anna Holloway-Attorney at Law. The card also offers an address for the law firm, 200 Park Boulevard, Suite Nine, Philadelphia, PA. It is this address that will be his destination. He must find Anna Holloway. For only she can provide the answers he is seeking…only she can help him get his life back.

The afternoon sun has now given way to cloud-covered skies as Patrick Hartley travels the final ten or so miles of the expressway to the merge point of the Pennsylvania Turnpike. A rain begins to fall, giving the pavement in front of him a glossy, polished appearance. Although he tries to stay focused on what's ahead of him, he can't help but begin to daydream about a reunion with his wife and child. Will he be able to find them?...what would it be like to see their faces after all these years?...would he recognize them? Although these questions fill him with nervous apprehension, he is more than willing to press on, realizing he can't afford to let fear cost him any more than it already has. Hope and faith will be his guide...love for his family that he feels deep in his heart...even though memory still eludes him...this love will show him the way...this much he believes...he must have hope...hope is all he has.

As Patrick stares straight ahead at the road in front of him, almost lulled into trance by the headlights of approaching vehicles, he is rudely startled out of his daydream. The hairs on the back of his neck seem to stand at attention and goose bumps appear down the length of both arms. His forehead breaks out in sweat as he grips the wheel tighter now. Before he can even think about his actions, he jerks the wheel suddenly to the right. The vehicle swings wildly off the expressway and onto the shoulder of the road, narrowly missing the guardrail. He slams on the brakes and sits there frozen in silence, his mind spinning in terror. Like a speeding freight train, memories pass through him.

In his mind he sees the headlights…a vehicle racing toward him…he hears the screams. He can almost feel the tires locking…he recalls the mile marker sign. Just as quickly as the terrifying memory appears, it is all-at-once gone. Patrick snaps back into reality. A rush of relief moves through him as he realizes he is still sitting there on the shoulder of the road. As he stares out the windshield of the green Toyota, he is not at all surprised to see the sign there in front of him…mile marker 224. "My god, it was right here", he says out loud. "I remember it now…it happened right here!"

He recalls now the conversation he had with Stadnik, "…more memories will return over time, Mr. Hartley. Some of these memories will terrify you…worse than any nightmare you can imagine." Patrick continues to stare at the mile marker sign for another few minutes, breathing deeply and trying to compose himself. Finally, he puts the vehicle back into gear and presses on. As he stares ahead down the rain-soaked expressway, he wonders what is waiting for him down the road. It seems to him that the dark rain clouds ahead are symbolic somehow…as if he has reached a point of no return. He resigns himself to the fact that there

are countless dangers ahead and many horrible
memories still to recall. He also reminds himself
that, just like any rainstorm, there are clearer skies
ahead. These dark clouds he must pass through to
reach his destiny…clearer skies are surely ahead.
Somewhere out there is Anna Holloway. He must
find her and learn what she already knows. The
truth is out there on the horizon. Patrick Hartley
grips the wheel tightly, guiding the Toyota through
the rain…and focuses his mind on the task at hand.

11

Dr. Leo Stadnik rubs his tired, bloodshot eyes and strokes his thin, dark mustache. He is seated at the desk in the corner of the make-shift hospital room in the basement of the yellow house in Wildwood, New Jersey. Ever since this nightmare has begun, he has spent seemingly endless days and nights sitting at this desk. He reads and rereads file after file of information related to the project and, more specifically, about the life and work of Owen Darden. Surely there was something he missed, some sort of clue.

Stadnik seems forever lost in a struggle to understand it all. Slowly, it seems to eat away at him like an infection. He was once so proud of who he was...he once believed in his cause. He remembers an afternoon when his car was stopped at a red light and a busload of school children filed off the bus. He remembered their faces and thinking to himself, this is the reason I do what I do. Because of people like him, those kids will grow up, get married, and have a family…a future…because of people like him. It turns his stomach to think of it now. He wants now to find those children and tell them he is sorry…beg their forgiveness and tell them he failed…he can't protect them…no one can.

He recalls his first meeting with Dr. Darden. He remembers being so impressed with the man. He once regarded him as a hero with a brilliant mind. There is no doubt that Owen Darden was a brilliant man. Unfortunately, as Dr. Stadnik has come to learn, this type of brilliance comes at a price. Sometimes, the exceptionally bright walk such a fine line between intelligent and eccentric, wise and foolish. Sometimes these lines are easy to distinguish. Stadnik had come across those types before and was always skilled at reading them. In Special Agent Training in Quantico, he was taught how to spot deception. Eye touching, neck touching, turning the body away, too much eye contact or not enough…the instructor used to say a good agent needs to develop a sixth sense.

Something in the eyes, he used to tell everyone, something in the eyes always gives people away. Stadnik recalls staring directly into the eyes of Owen Darden and seeing no signs of deception or anything disturbing. The man seemed so determined, his cause so righteous. He had a certain effect on those around him that was difficult to describe. He had an ability to draw people in, to make them believers, to make them want to share his vision. Dr. Stadnik was one of those believers. He allowed this man to manipulate him…him and everyone else. How could this man who seemed so wise and good turn his back and side with everything that is wrong with the world? Even worse, how did he, Dr. Leo Stadnik, allow this to happen? This is the constant battle he fights within his conscience and he vows to set things right again. Starting with Patrick Hartley, but it will not end with him. Stadnik has vowed to find them all and give them what they deserve…their lives back. But how many are there? When will it all end? It's a dreadful thought that he doesn't even want to contemplate. How far is Darden prepared to go? Is it too late to stop them? He pictures a dark and horrible world where armies of manipulated half-humans carry out countless acts of violence on innocent lives.

Stadnik recalls a day that he stood alongside Owen Darden in a room inside the White House. That day, Darden was able to shake hands with the president. He looked everyone in the eye, including the president, telling them the history of the world was about to change. That remark seemed filled with such hope and promise on that day. Now, it seems as if it was an ominous warning from a madman. Stadnik wonders how he can ever face his own wife and child again. He wonders how he can try to explain this to all of them…how he can convince them that he thought he was doing something for the greater good. How can he look his own child in the eye and tell him that he's helped to jeopardize his future? He realizes that the events and decisions of the past can't be changed. The only thing that he can do is try to set things right. It may be too late to stop it, but he is aware that he is the one person who can give them a chance. He needs to be able to look himself in the mirror again, to pick up the broken pieces of his own life and salvage something. He feels little peace from the actions he has taken with Patrick Hartley. He tried to remain optimistic when he spoke to him, telling him that he could make a difference…telling him he could find his family. In truth, he doesn't hold out much hope for him. The reality is that Patrick Hartley is now a marked man. Releasing him from his prison of mind control will likely not save him. In all probability, he might not last a day out there. Darden and the others will search endlessly for him and they will find him. Even by some slim chance his family is still alive, they will also be in grave danger. Knowing the kind of people that Darden has surrounded himself with, they will leave nothing to chance. As Stadnik gathers up the papers to place them back into the manila folders, he hears footsteps upstairs. His partner, Dr. Felton, has finally arrived.

Tonight, they will be leaving the yellow house for good. With the release of Hartley, their work here is done. They will move on now, in search of the others. Stadnik takes one final deep breath before grabbing up the folders and pushing himself away from the work desk. He yells upstairs to Felton, "Ben, are you ready to go?" Not surprisingly, his partner doesn't respond. Although they have worked together for years, Stadnik still forgets about his partner's hearing problem. Eight years ago, Benjamin Felton was at the scene when a pipe bomb exploded in a bus terminal in upstate New York. Although he escaped with only minor injuries, the blast left Felton with partial deafness in both ears. Despite constant nagging from his partner and family members, Felton refuses to wear hearing aids. He is a man of deep pride, and one who refuses to acknowledge his shortcomings. On more than one occasion, Stadnik has nearly come to blows with his partner over this issue. Stadnik's contention is that he is putting both of their lives in danger by refusing to wear hearing aids. Felton always counters that what he lacks in hearing, he makes up for with his other senses. He has a ridiculous belief that his hearing deficiency has caused his other senses to develop into some super-human form. Stadnik has never seen any evidence of this while working with his partner. The discussion often ends with Stadnik merely rolling his eyes and shaking his head.

"Ben, you ready to go?" he calls again. Again, no response from his partner upstairs. As Stadnik begins to make his way upstairs, he yells a third time. This time, he is growing annoyed. "Ben, where the hell are you?" He hears no response but sees a figure at the top of the stairs. Although Stadnik is unable to recognize the face connected to the figure, he immediately senses that it is not his partner. As he turns in panic to run back down the stairs, a loud shot rings out. A thud echoes around the staircase as plaster rains down on him from above. Despite his best efforts to steady himself, Stadnik loses his footing, tumbling down the steps. He hits his head hard on the basement floor which dazes him slightly. When he's able to look up, he sees the figure standing over him now. He can also see the face, a face he knows all too well. The eyes that stare at him are eyes he has studied many times before. "You...what do you want?...what do you want from me?" A single gunshot to the head ends the life of Dr. Leo Stadnik.

12

Patrick Hartley sits in the parked car across the street from the tall office building on Park Boulevard in downtown Philadelphia. He holds the business card of Anna Holloway in his right hand, tapping it nervously against the stick shift of the Toyota Camry. He moves his eyes from the business card, then to the office building while simultaneously tapping his foot nervously on the vehicle's hard plastic floormat. It has been hours since he has eaten, and his stomach is producing audible sounds reminding him of this fact. Although he is hungry, eating would not be possible now given his flustered state. Upon arriving at his destination on Park Boulevard, his first instinct had been to immediately exit the vehicle and enter the building. Now, a growing uneasiness has come over him. While he is fully aware that he must find Anna Holloway, the frightening thought has occurred to him that he is probably not the only one searching for her. Based on the details Dr. Stadnik shared about the adversaries involved, Patrick's sudden hesitation seems justified. Another disturbing thought is that others may be looking for him as well. He thinks about the picture of the face from Atlantic City that Stadnik had shown him…the picture of his own face. If Dr. Stadnik and his partner were able to find him, why couldn't anyone else? The worst part of the dilemma for Patrick is having no idea whom to fear. Every face to him is a stranger, and therefore a potential enemy. Now convincing himself that making a move would be foolish, he decides to wait it out. His best hope, he decides, is to wait for Anna Holloway to emerge. Unfortunately, the brief description Stadnik offered is not much to go on…blonde, attractive, mid-twenties. In a city of this size, in a building of this size for that matter, he doesn't like his chances of recognizing her. He curses to himself in frustration. He asks himself what he is doing here…why is this happening to him? He throws the business card onto the passenger's seat of the Camry in disgust and leans his head back against the headrest. As he stares up at the vehicle's plastic dome-light, his eyes begin to grow heavy. He shakes his head and shuffles in his seat. He tells himself that he must stay awake…he must not sleep. Despite his battle to remain alert, sleep finally wins.

Amid dreams, memories present themselves to Patrick Hartley. In fast-moving frames, like a flashing billboard…the memories flicker around relentlessly in his mind. In one of these frames, he is crouched in a bush staring in the window of what appears to be a convenience store. In the next frame, a man stares at him with terror in his eyes. In yet another scene, he is outside…a warm ocean breeze blows steadily around him. This time a more detailed and terrifying recollection. He is clutching the younger man, lifting him off his feet as the man screams in terror.

With a violent jolt, Hartley awakens from this dream, soaked in sweat and pulse racing. He is at first completely disoriented, lost somewhere between fantasy and reality. Only after a short time elapses does he realize where he is…still seated in the vehicle on Park Boulevard. In a sudden rush of panic, Patrick turns the vehicle's ignition to display the digital clock in the dashboard. The display reads 5:47pm. He is relieved to discover that he has only been asleep for twenty minutes or so. He glances out the window and sees that the evening rush has begun. A steady stream of seemingly hundreds of pedestrians pass by the Camry. Some are walking, some are running to catch buses and cabs. He moves his eyes back to the office building across the street, now fearing that he may have missed Anna Holloway while he slept. He curses and scolds himself repeatedly for falling asleep. Just as a feeling of complete hopelessness is falling upon him, a woman emerges from the building.

She is dressed in a navy-blue business suit and carries a black handbag. She is also blonde, very attractive, and appears to be someone around her mid-twenties…she perfectly matches Dr. Stadnik's description. Without hesitation this time, Patrick opens the door and jumps out of the vehicle, leaving the keys still in the ignition. A nervous excitement comes over him as he waits for the street light to change so he can cross. He steps swiftly down the sidewalk, waiting until he is just a few feet behind her before calling out to her. "Excuse me Miss, may I speak with you a moment?" The young woman turns toward Patrick with a startled look. "Anna Holloway?...are you Anna Holloway?" Suddenly, the face of the young woman changes. Her complexion seems to turn pale white and a look of panic crosses her face, as if she has seen a ghost or the devil himself. "Who are you...what do you want?" she asks. "Please Miss, I need to know...are you Anna Holloway?" The woman pauses before answering. "I'm not...no, you have the wrong person." With that she turns and begins to walk away. "Please, I need to find Anna Holloway." She turns around again to look at him. This time, Patrick sees tears beginning to form in the young woman's eyes. "What is this about?" she asks him. "I can't tell you that, can you please tell me where I can find her. It's an emergency." The young woman's voice begins to crack as she answers him. " Anna is...dead." They stand there in silence for a moment, each of them waiting for the other to speak. Tears are now running down the woman's cheeks. Patrick tries to respond but can only utter the words..."What?...how?...when?" The woman continues to sob, uncontrollably now. "She was killed...shot and killed. It happened just the other day...right over there." She points her finger, motioning further down the street. "Do they know who killed her" Hartley asks. "No" the woman replies. "I...I can't help you anymore. Why were you looking for her?" Patrick pauses for a moment before answering. "Business…legal business actually…I needed to see her about some legal business. The woman nods her head slowly, tears still streaming down her face. "You knew her well? Patrick asks. "Yes, very well. We went to law school together. We lived together for two years." Patrick can see that the woman is terribly distraught. Despite this, he must press her for answers. "Did she have any family here in Philadelphia?" The woman lowers her head to avoid eye contact. "Listen, I told you…I can't help you." Patrick presses on, realizing this may be his only chance. " May I at least have one of your business cards then? Perhaps you could help me with my legal matter." The woman turns and begins walking away as she answers. "Look mister…if you need an appointment, you need to come into the office during business hours. This conversation is over." With that, the woman continues down the sidewalk…leaving Patrick standing there alone and hopeless.

Patrick Hartley walks slowly back to the green Toyota Camry, still parked with the keys in the ignition. His head hangs low and his eyes stare at the sidewalk. He feels as if a dark cloud is right above him now. With his hope of finding Anna Holloway dashed, so is the hope of finding answers about his wife and child. While it is possible that Anna Holloway would have had nothing to offer in the way of information, it is equally possible that she had everything to offer. This is the thought that scares him...an opportunity has been lost...perhaps his only opportunity. He arrives at the vehicle to find it has not been disturbed...perhaps surprisingly considering the keys were left in the ignition and the doors were unlocked. As Patrick climbs back into the driver's seat, the hopelessness of his situation hits him like a lead pipe across the skull. He grips the steering wheel with both hands and curses loudly. He sits there motionless as seconds pass by, attempting to refocus his anger and formulate a plan. Dusk has arrived and darkness soon will follow. He must accept the fact that, if there is a breakthrough on the horizon, it will not happen on this day. He must find a place to stay for the night. He reaches into the glove box and pulls out the envelope that Stadnik had given him. He checks the contents of the envelope and finds that cash is still inside. In his mad rush to follow the young woman, he had forgotten about the money in the glove box. He scolds himself again, this time for his carelessness, and reminds himself that there is no room for any more errors. He must give up for the night and find a place to sleep. Tomorrow is a new day, he tries to tell himself.

13

Beverly Holloway sits at the picnic bench and watches the little girl enjoying her ice cream. The child had insisted on an adult-sized cherry-dipped cone about the size of her entire face. Although more than half of the ice cream seems to be ending up on the girl's pretty, yellow shirt, Bev is savoring every moment of watching this adorable spectacle. It's funny the way ice cream has such an effect on a child. Beverly can't help but reflect on the happy times with Anna at this very ice cream stand. Whether disappointed about not making the cheerleading squad, a fight with a best friend, or a bad hairdo…ice cream was always the cure. It seems to her only yesterday that her beautiful young Anna sat there, five feet away in that pretend fire truck at Charley's Ice Cream.

It's hard to believe she is gone. It's impossible to comprehend and so unfair. She hasn't yet begun to come to terms with her loss, nor does she know if she ever will. The shock has not worn off, and Beverly is just trying to cope the best that she can, one day at a time. Yesterday, the family held a small vigil for Anna at the funeral parlor in Center City Philadelphia. Beverly would have loved to have a proper viewing and funeral, but the horrible truth is that the location of the bullet which caused her daughter's fatal injuries made this impossible. Beverly instead made the difficult decision to have her daughter cremated. She will at least have a part of her daughter with her, in a beautiful urn up on the mantle in the family room back at the house in King of Prussia, PA. This is not much of a conciliation to Beverly. She has lost her precious daughter, and for what? Who would do something like this? Who would want to hurt her? Yes, Anna was an attorney, and not everyone she encountered was a good person. The police suspect that her job did play a factor, and they continue to investigate the cases Anna was involved with and the people she interacted with in the days and hours before the shooting. The officers did warn that they may never find her killer. Witnesses were questioned, but none of them could say for sure where the bullet came from, and no one was able to identify a suspect. Despite the police wanting to ask questions and dig into everything and everyone that Anna knew, Beverly doesn't see much of a point in it. Her daughter is not coming home, and the person who ended her life will have to answer to god. She chooses instead to remember her daughter for the beautiful, kind, and gentle person she was.

At the service in the funeral home, so many of Anna's friends and colleagues had approached Beverly. They spoke of her determination and perseverance. They spoke so highly of her as a person of both internal and external beauty. As Bev would look into their eyes, she could truly see that they were sincere. Anna did also have an ultra-competitive side to be sure. Beverly is not naïve enough to think that some of these people who spoke so highly of Anna may also have crossed paths with her in some negative way. Her daughter was the second most competitive person she knew, her husband and Anna's father Frank being the first.

Bev recalls the way that Anna's father pushed her from a very young age. When something would go wrong for her, he refused to allow her to whine about it. He taught her that everyone falls a time or two…but it is the special ones who pick themselves up, dust themselves off, and try harder next time. Sometimes Bev would argue with her husband about being too hard on Anna. She is, after all, a girl Beverly would argue. Frank's response to her was always the same. He would always respond by saying that there are billions of people in this world and that only the strong survive. He would insist that treating her softly as a child would only encourage this behavior in her adult life. "The population keeps growing" he would say to her, "soon there will be no more room in the world for the weak." To hear someone talk this way, one might wonder how a person like Beverly would end up with this type of man. For all his tough talk though, Frank Holloway was a kind and gentle soul. He was raised in a rural part of West Virginia and was the son of a coal miner who died of black lung, an illness acquired from spending years in the mines. His father died when Frank was only twelve years old, leaving him to care for his younger brother and sister. Frank used to tell Beverly and Anna stories of how his father would go to work every day, despite being almost too sick to walk. Back in those days he would remind them, there was no such thing as sick time or disability. Back then, if a person wanted to eat…and he wanted his family to eat…he worked, plain and simple. This would explain where her husband's toughness came from and his belief in commitment and perseverance. These are the traits which he passed along to Anna. Along with these traits, he also passed on another important belief…a belief in helping others. Several times when Anna was a child, Frank would take the family back to the small town where he was born in Monongah, West Virginia. He would load up the car with boxes of canned goods and old toys to share with the less fortunate residents there. During these visits, he would not only drop the boxes off and leave; he would stay and talk with the people. He would offer them advice and comfort when he could. People seemed to trust him and believe in him. This belief in helping others was another trait he passed on to Anna. She helped anyone in need. Although her chosen profession of attorney might seem to some a contradiction, this would not be a fair assessment. Anna truly believed in what she did. She believed that a person was innocent until proven guilty. Most of all, she believed in second chances. Although

Beverly has no idea what lies in store for the little ice-cream covered girl sitting across from her, she would never dream of turning her back on her. To do so would be an insult to Anna and everything she stood for. This little girl is someone in need...someone who needs and deserves a second chance.

"I'm all done" the little girl proclaims, suddenly jolting Beverly from her deep thoughts and back into reality. The young girl smiles at her with an ice-cream covered grin. "You're ready to go then?" asks Bev. "Yes ma'am, all ready." With that, the child jumps off the pretend fire engine and reaches for Beverly's hand. Bev is overcome for a moment by the overwhelming sweetness of the child...a sweetness that reminds her so much of her precious Anna. She fights off tears that are starting to form in her eyes. "Let's go then, I hope you are still able to eat some dinner later after that giant ice cream cone." The little girl then explains to her, as only a child can, that only the dessert part of her stomach is full. The child points to the left side of her belly. "See, only this side is full...this is the side of my stomach where ice cream and candy go." The girl then points to the right side of her stomach…"on this side is where the good for you food goes . See, this side is empty." Beverly gives the child a warm smile…"guess you can't argue with that logic. Let's go little one."

The two of them walk together in the direction of Beverly's blue Dodge Caravan. Bev recalls the day when she came home from the dealership with the minivan. Anna was home for the holidays and came out into the driveway to greet her. She smiles to herself as she recalls Anna, standing there with her arms folded and frowning. "Oh please, Mom…a minivan? That's an old lady's car. You'll never meet a man driving in that thing." Beverly responded by saying she's already met a wonderful man. "He was the best man in the world, your father. He might be gone but he is still with me and that's all I'll ever need."

As Beverly and the young girl arrive at the vehicle, the child spots a man with a ball cap standing in the parking lot next to a white van. The man is holding up a colorful array of balloons and smiles as he hands them out to a group of children. The little girl releases her grip on Beverly's hand and starts immediately in his direction. "Where do you think you are going, little one?" The little girl pleads with Beverly. "Oh please…can I get a red balloon?" Unable to say no to the little girl, Beverly agrees. "One red balloon, then we have to go." She follows the child up to the man who stares back at them smiling. Bev smiles back at the man and asks if they can please have a red balloon. "Yes, you certainly can. There you go little one." He starts to hand the balloon to the little girl, then hesitates. He hands the balloon to Beverly. "You should tie it on her wrist so that it doesn't blow away." As he steps between the two of them, the man whispers over his shoulder to Beverly. "They are coming for you." Beverly stares at him blankly, obvious confusion on her face. "What are you talking about, who is coming?" The man looks into Beverly eyes now and whispers. "They can't know I'm talking to you…you need to take her…you need to take her and leave…leave before they find you." Beverly pulls the child back toward her, now in a state of panic. "What are you talking about? Who are you?" The man continues, "You've been warned…if I found you, they can find you too" With that, he carries the balloons over to the van. Just as he arrives at the side of the van, the side doors slide open. The man dives into the van and the vehicle speeds off in a cloud of dirt before the doors even have time to close. The little girl looks up at Beverly innocently. "Who was that man?...What was he talking about?" Beverly stares back at the little girl, trying her best to appear calm. "I don't know, sweetie. He...he thought we were someone else I guess. Yes, that's all...he thought we were someone else.

14

Patrick Hartley sits on the edge of the bed inside his room at the bed and breakfast. He looks over to the mirror above the large dresser in front of him, attempting to focus his eyes on his reflection. He stretches, yawns deeply, and rubs the sleep out of his eyes. The previous evening, instead of returning to Philadelphia, he had chosen to drive across the Ben Franklin Bridge to Camden, New Jersey. He chose Camden only because it was the first town name he had seen on the map he purchased from a gas station somewhere just outside of downtown Philly. He decided to rely on fate and drive to the first town he saw, despite a rather ominous warning from the cashier at the gas station. When the man had asked Patrick where he was headed and he answered Camden, the man seemed less than fond of the town. "You know buddy, Camden was once named the most dangerous city in the United States." As he handed Hartley his change he continued…"anyone looking to stay in Camden is either running away from trouble or looking to find some." Patrick simply tried to ignore the man and accept his change, but the man insisted on continuing. "I think you're in luck though. I think this year Camden fell down to like sixth on the list of most dangerous cities…so I guess there are five other worse places to be than there, right buddy?" Patrick couldn't help but wonder to himself if one of those five places was right here talking to this man. He chose instead to ignore him, nodding and smiling as he turned and headed back to his car. He decided that Camden would still be his destination. He has only himself to rely on now, and he has only his instincts and fate to guide him.

Patrick had driven for more than twenty minutes through the town of Camden before settling on a place to stay. Although he found the city at nighttime to be about as inviting as the man at the gas station had described it, he did manage to find a place that didn't look too terrible. Just on the outskirts of town, he settled on a place called The Winchester, with a sign describing it as a

Victorian Gothic Bed and Breakfast. When he stepped inside, the interior was old, a little dark, but surprisingly clean. It would do just fine for the evening. After checking in and paying cash, he had retired to his room for the night. He had fallen asleep quickly and managed to have a restful night's sleep , free from any dreams good or bad. He has awakened refreshed and ready to continue. Although yesterday he was devasted by the turn of events regarding Anna Holloway, he has started the day with a more positive feeling and a destination in mind. This morning, he decided he will return to Mile Marker 224…where it all began. He had felt something on his last visit there…a spark of memory…but even more than that a feeling that the location has more to show him. He must continue to believe in fate…and he must continue to have faith because it's all he has now. He stares at his reflection in the mirror for a final moment and reminds himself to stay focused and stay positive. Finally, he proclaims out loud, "Let's go find your family."

While checking out of his room at the front desk, a friendly woman working there suggested he have breakfast in the small dining room. Until she had mentioned food, Patrick hadn't thought about how hungry he is, but his stomach has reminded him. He agrees and heads down the hallway to a small dining room with only four tables covered in simple, white cloth. The walls of the dining room contain a lot of photos and memorabilia, mostly black and white, showing the town of Camden, New Jersey in its glory days. Other photos show random people, young and old, standing out in front of the bed and breakfast. Former guests apparently from many eras, some smiling brightly, others very stern looking. Other than one female employee in the dining room, there is a young couple seated at the table next to him. They smile warmly at Patrick and bid him good morning. Hartley nods and smiles in return. The young female, a cute young brunette who appears to be in her early twenties, is the more talkative one. She can't wait to tell Patrick the news of her recent engagement, bursting with happiness as she shows him the round-cut diamond on her ring finger. "We just got engaged last night!...sorry I'm just so excited I have to tell everyone!" Patrick smiles and congratulates the young couple, despite a hint of sadness that has come over him. The young woman senses it and asked him if everything is ok. "Yes" Patrick says, "Seeing you two just makes me miss my wife and family." For the first time, the young man speaks, "Are you away on business or something?" Patrick attempts to keep his composure as he answers. "No, I'm going to see them soon... I have a lot of lost time to make up for...but I'm going to see them soon."

The traffic is relatively light along the Atlantic City Expressway. Luckily, Patrick has missed the worst of the morning rush hour. It takes him a little under an hour to arrive at his destination, mile marker 224. He had gone two exits past and then circled back onto the expressway to the east-bound side, feeling that it was important to recreate the exact trip he had taken on that fateful night. As he had completed the last mile to the site of the accident, he had prepared himself, and even hoped for, some spark of memory as he had experienced the previous afternoon. This time, however, not even an inkling of memory has appeared. Patrick decides to park his car on the shoulder of the highway and walk over to the guardrail, hoping something will jar his memory. He stands still at the mile marker sign and closes his eyes, listening to the swoosh of passing cars go by. He focuses his mind and tries to put himself back there again…trying to imagine the scene. The rain…the headlights…"come on Patrick…remember…you need to remember." He is so intently fixated on trying to conjure up the memory that he is not immediately aware of the vehicle that has pulled off the highway and onto the shoulder, stopping directly in front of the Camry.

When Patrick opens his eyes, he sees a black Mercedes with windows so darkly tinted that the two figures inside are merely silhouettes. Quickly, the two men exit the vehicle and walk briskly toward him. Both men are dressed in dark suits and wear black, mirrored sunglasses. The one on the right has lighter hair and is taller. The shorter one on the left is the first to speak…"stay right where you are Hartley…don't even try to run." Just then, a horn sounds from another vehicle and Patrick sees a tan Lexus swerve off the highway, nearly side swiping the Camry and sending both dark-suited men diving over the guardrail for cover. The Lexus stops next to Patrick and the driver kicks open the passenger door. There is only one man in the vehicle, an older man with a pencil-thin mustache. Patrick also notices that the man is wearing the same kind of sweater that Stadnik wore. "Get in if you want to stay alive!" the man shouts. Patrick hesitates momentarily, as he quickly glances over at the two men in dark suits struggling to get back to their feet. "Let's go!...those guys are going to kill you!...get in!" Patrick goes with his first instinct and jumps into the Lexus. The driver launches the car forward before Patrick can even close the passenger door. Without hesitation, the driver swerves the vehicle back onto the highway, nearly missing the rear-end of a yellow taxi.

"Hold on and keep your head down" the driver says as he recklessly changes lanes. Patrick ducks down low in the passenger seat and remains speechless. He looks over at the driver who is nervously checking the rearview mirror. Finally, Patrick regains his composure enough to speak…"who are you?...who were those guys?...what is happening?" The man glances over at Patrick, then back to the road. "Just keep your head down…I'm a little busy right now." Then, in a quick jerking motion, the driver moves the vehicle back onto the shoulder of the road and hits the accelerator. Patrick glances over at the speedometer and sees that they are now traveling at speeds approaching ninety miles per hour. Once again stunned speechless, he covers his eyes with his hands and ducks down even lower in the passenger seat. Continuing to drive on the shoulder of the road, the driver then shoots down an exit ramp. He makes a sharp right turn at the bottom of the ramp, steering the vehicle off the shoulder of the road and down a long, gravel driveway. At the bottom of the driveway is what looks like an old, abandoned repair shop. Two rusted-out junk cars are parked in front with doors and tires missing. A half-dozen or so hubcaps and old, rusty oil cans are sitting off to the side of the two closed garage doors. The driver pulls the vehicle to the back of the garage and kills the ignition. Finally, Patrick speaks…"Where are we?...what is happening?...who are you?" The man looks over at Patrick and raises his hand to silence him. "Wait here for a second." The man then gets out of the car and walks cautiously to the side of garage. He peers around the corner in the direction of the gravel driveway. Apparently satisfied, he walks back to the vehicle and climbs back into the driver's side. "Looks like we've lost them. It's alright, we are safe here for a while." After a brief period of silence, the man looks over at Patrick. "I know who you are, Mr. Hartley, and I know you are wondering who I am. You were with my partner yesterday, Dr. Stadnik." Patrick is then able to put some of the pieces together. "So you are Dr. Felton. Stadnik mentioned you…where is Stadnik?" Felton looks away from Hartley and stares out the window. "Dr. Stadnik is dead…he was shot and killed yesterday." Patrick shakes his head, "no, that's impossible, I was with him yesterday." Felton looks back over at Hartley, then stares back out the window, seemingly unable to maintain eye contact. "I'm aware of that" Felton continues, "he was shot and killed only a short time after you left. Now it is Patrick who stares out the window. "Who killed him?" Felton turns his head to meet Patrick's eyes once again. "The same people who are trying to kill you, Mr. Hartley."

Patrick puts his head back and exhales deeply. He is suddenly exhausted and unable to stand another minute of this. He has grown tired of hearing about death and hopelessness. Although there are a million questions he wants to ask Dr. Felton, he is speechless. As if one more negative word or thought will shatter him, he chooses to sit in silence for a moment longer. Felton seems to sense the emotion and allows Patrick time to gather his thoughts before he speaks. "Listen, Mr. Hartley, there are a lot of people who would love nothing more to go back in time and change things. I am one of them. I worked with Dr. Stadnik for so many years that I considered him almost a brother. As much as I'd like things to be different, we are where we are. We all knew the risks involved and were aware of the worst-case scenarios. I don't think any of us believed it would happen, but it has. There are people out there who wish the world harm and we can't let them win." At this point, all Patrick can do is laugh. "No offense, Dr. Felton, but it looks like they are definitely winning. What reaction am I supposed to have to this? Your mistakes have cost me my life...they have cost me my family. Are you aware of Anna Holloway? Do you know that she is dead too? I'm guessing you probably are. I tried to track her down yesterday and instead ran into her best friend and former roommate. She told me that someone killed Anna in broad daylight, right down the street from her office. I'm sure you also know that finding Anna Holloway alive might have been my only hope of ever finding my family. She knew something according to what Dr. Stadnik told me. Now I'll never know what she knew. So how can you sit there and say we can't let them win?...they've already won." Felton pauses, as if making sure Patrick is finished before speaking. "First of all, Mr. Hartley, you are still alive. Those guys back there, they want you dead…they want all of us dead…but we are still alive. I'm going to make sure you stay alive. I intend to see this through…and you are going to see this through with me, Hartley. First, you are going to need one of these.." Felton reaches over Patrick and opens the glove compartment. He pulls out a handgun and drops it in Hartley's lap. "Now, there is someone we need to go see…someone who can help us. With that, Felton starts the car, makes a U-turn, and heads back up the gravel driveway.

15

It was no surprise that Beverly Holloway had a problem getting the young girl to sleep. When they had returned to the house in King of Prussia, the child was nowhere near ready for bed. After the mountain of ice cream she had recently consumed, complete with cherry dip, the child was riding a sugar high that seemed would last a lifetime. Beverly had forgotten how exhausting little ones can be to handle at times, especially for a woman in her sixties. The little girl had begged to stay up and watch her favorite program on the Disney Channel. As a compromise, Beverly agreed to read the girl a story instead. She selected a book of fairly-tales that Anna kept in her bedroom from childhood. Anna's favorite story was Cinderella, so it seemed only fitting that Bev chose this one to read to the child.

They crawled into Anna's bad, where the child had slept the last several nights. Although it was difficult for Beverly to be in her daughter's room so soon, surrounded by so many memories of her daughter, she had chosen to have the little girl sleep there. The room is on the second floor of the big, old house, just one door away from Bev's bedroom. This way, she felt secure that the child was close by in case she woke up scared in the night. Beverly was also concerned about how the child was handling everything that has happened. Earlier in the day, the little girl had asked a question that brought Bev to tears.. "Is Anna really up in heaven with the angels?" Beverly had tried to explain things to the child, trying to think of the best way to do so in a way that the little girl would understand. She told her that Anna was not coming home again. She explained to her that Anna was needed in heaven and had gone to be with the angels. Tears formed in the child's eyes when she told her this, but she never cried. Beverly was amazed by the child's strength, a strength that reminded her so much of Anna. She was concerned though as well. Obviously, this sweet and innocent child had seen more than her share of tragedy and was holding up remarkably well…but how much tragedy can a young child take?

As the story of Cinderella was ending, Bev could see the eyes of the young girl growing heavy. To her surprise and delight, the child seemed to enjoy the story almost as much as Anna had. The child had sat there, absorbing every word, as Bev read how the fairy godmother turned the pumpkin into a coach, mice into horses, a rat into a coachman, and lizards into footmen. The little girl smiled at the same parts of the story Anna used to…when Cinderella returns to the palace and marries the prince…and the best part of all…when the wicked stepsisters begged her forgiveness. Finally drifting off to sleep, the young child looks up at Bev and smiles. "I hope I meet a handsome prince one day. Beverly leans down and kisses the little girl on the forehead. "You will little princess…you will." Beverly pulls the covers over the child and watches her sleep a little while longer before picking the book up off the bed and placing it back on the shelf. She turns on the night light and quietly shuts the door.

Bev walks quietly down the upstairs hallway, pausing at the top of the stairs and looking down at the living room below. She has always loved this house. She clearly remembers when they first brought Anna home from the hospital. She remembers her little girl, crawling across that same living room floor like it was only yesterday. Because of these beautiful memories, she knows she will never leave. So much has changed with the outside world, but the home looks much the same as when Anna was born. Although her husband worked in the city, they had chosen to settle here and raise their family. They chose this town with the peculiar name, King of Prussia, a quiet place close to Philly. The town has changed quite a bit since then. Over twenty-thousand people now call this city home. It is also home to one of the largest malls in the United States. The mall attracts shoppers from all over, increasing traffic and costing the city some of its small-town charm. Still, this city is home…it will always be home.

Beverly walks down the stairs toward the living room, stepping quietly to avoid waking the sleeping child. She stops at the bottom of the staircase, turns on the small lamp by the sofa, and proceeds to the kitchen. She has decided to finish the evening with a glass of wine. She has never been much of a drinker. The Holloways have never been a family of drinkers. Her late husband Frank used to enjoy the occasional drink of Brandy on holidays, a tradition passed on from his old English relatives. Lately though, Beverly does enjoy a good glass of white wine before bed. With all the turmoil that has happened in her life recently, anything to help her sleep can't be a bad thing. She reaches onto the top shelf of the kitchen cupboard for a wine glass, then turns to reach the bottle on the counter. That's when it catches her eye, through the kitchen window right above the sink, something…someone in the backyard. It happens so quickly, just a shadow…she can't be sure. She walks over to the door that leads from the kitchen to the backyard and switches on the outdoor light. She stares out the window, scanning the part of backyard she can see from inside but sees nothing. Still, she is certain that something was there. Suddenly, an imaginary alarm begins to sound in her mind. She recalls the warning from the man with the balloons. She had tried to forget it…tried to believe that he truly did have her confused with someone else. Now, she is in a state of panic. What if someone is out there? What if someone is trying to harm her…or worse yet, harm the child?

With her hand shaking uncontrollably, she

switches off the outdoor light and stands in the kitchen, frozen in fear. She talks to herself, trying to formulate a plan. "Pick up the phone…who do I call?…I'll call the police…but what do I tell them?…I think I saw something…Or maybe I'll tell them about the man with the balloons. Oh Beverly, stop it!…you're being ridiculous." After about another minute of this, she decides that she is indeed just being paranoid. She forces herself to snap out of it and go back to what she was doing. She reaches for the wine glass again, this time even more eager for a drink to calm her nerves. As she reaches for the bottle, she hears a noise at the front door…someone is trying to open the door.

Her legs have become weak with fright…her heart is racing in terror. There is no time to call anyone. She can only think one thing…protect the little girl. Without hesitation or concern for her own safety, she runs back into the living room and up the stairs, two at a time. As she reaches the second floor, the sound at the front door grows much louder. It sounds as though someone is now kicking at the door, trying to break it down. She runs down the upstairs hallway toward Anna's room and the sleeping child.

Beverly kicks open the bedroom door. Almost simultaneously, she hears the front door open downstairs. She runs as fast she can over to the bed and grabs the little girl...just as she hears footsteps in the living room downstairs. "It's okay sweetie, we've got to go." The child wakes up frightened now and calls out..."what's going on?" Beverly covers the little girl's mouth to muffle her screams. "Please honey, we need to be quiet." She hears the footsteps moving through the downstairs...more than one pair of footsteps now...and one of them is headed for the staircase. It's Beverly now who cries out in terror..."Oh please lord, someone help us!" She then hears a car door slam outside the front of the house. She hears the voices of two men downstairs. The car door has startled them, and she hears one man say to the other, "there's a car outside...someone is coming!" The other man says, "Let's go...out the back door." She hears footsteps and the kitchen door open...then silence.

16

Benjamin Felton moves the Lexus steadily down the Pennsylvania Turnpike as Patrick Hartley sits in the passenger seat, staring out the window in silence. They have been travelling for more than forty minutes without either man uttering a single syllable. Although Patrick is unsure of where Felton is taking him, he cannot muster up the energy to question their destination. Patrick's run-in with the two would-be assassins earlier in the day has left him emotionally and physically exhausted. Felton, on the other hand, has never been much for small talk. He has always been described as a quiet man by nature and somewhat of a loner. This quiet demeaner is interpreted by some as dignified, and others as arrogant and aloof. In truth, he wasn't always a quiet person. The years have made him that way. The things he has seen in his line of work, the unimaginable human suffering, and terrible deeds that man is capable of, have made him this way.

As he glances over at Hartley sitting there next to him, he can't help but feel sorry for the man. Although he has played a significant role in the events that put this man here...a man with no past and almost certainly no future, he never meant him any harm. Felton did what he was told to do...what he thought he had to do. Decisions made for the greater good always come with consequences, he realizes this and accepts it. He has always been aware of this price. This doesn't make him any less sympathetic to Patrick Hartley's case, but faced with the same scenario again, he would act the same. The fact is that no one could have foreseen the situation with Owen Darden and all the problems that followed. The only thing they can do now is deal with the present, wherever that leads them.

Felton glances over at Hartley again, and notices this time Hartley is staring back at him and preparing to break the silence. "What happened to your ears?" Patrick asks him, referring to the hearing aids Felton wears on both the left and right side. Felton pauses for a moment before answering. "Let's just say I was in the wrong place at the wrong time…story of my life." Felton looks away and continues driving, hoping this explanation will suffice. "You don't like to talk much, do you Felton?" Felton smiles and drops his guard for the moment. "My wife used to tell me that all the time. I guess there is no harm in telling you. About eight years ago, I was working as a Port Authority cop in New York City. I was working a detail at a bus station and we were short-handed. We received a report of a suspicious looking device that was found in a crowded part of the terminal. We should have called it in…we should have waited…but we didn't. My partner and I went to investigate the device which turned out to be a pipe bomb. Like I said, wrong place at the wrong time. Fortunately, I came out of it with only some permanent hearing loss. My partner wasn't so lucky, he was pronounced dead at the scene. Twenty-six years old…damned unfair. The worst part, they never caught the bastard. The world can be a sick place Mr. Hartley." Patrick turns his head away again to look out the window…."yeah, tell me about it."

They drive for an hour in total silence

before reaching an exit for the town of West Chester, Pennsylvania at 12:10pm. After turning off the exit, Felton makes two lefts, two rights, and pulls onto a small side street called Wilkins. Just a quarter mile down Wilkins, they pull into the parking lot of a run-down bar with a sign displaying Murphy's Pub. The tacky green awning on the front of the bar is warn and tattered. The sign over the door contains a green clover design, indicating that this is an Irish bar. Felton doesn't stop in the front parking lot, but instead drives to the rear of the building. They stop in front of an old wooden door in the back of the building. Felton puts the vehicle in park, then shuts off the engine. We're here, let's go." Patrick stares at the back of the building and asks, "who are we meeting here?" Felton doesn't answer him. He is already exiting the vehicle and walking toward the wooden door, motioning Hartley to follow him. Felton checks the door handle and finds that it is unlocked. The old door makes a loud creaking sound as he opens it, as if this door hasn't been used in years. The two men enter the storage area, a room filled with half-empty boxes filled with various types of booze. Felton leads them up a tiny staircase and into the bar area.

The room is poorly lit and contains a small jukebox on the right-hand side and a small pool table near the rear of the bar. The odor of the place is almost unbearable, reeking of both stale beer and old cigarettes. The only other person in the bar is seated at the far end and facing the doorway. The man sees Felton and Hartley approaching and waves them over to him. "Dr. Felton, I've been waiting for you. Come have a beer gentlemen, this is my bother-in-law's place." Patrick studies the man at the bar. He looks to be in his early forties, with slightly graying hair and an unshaven face. He seems as though he could be a handsome man were it not for his disheveled appearance. There is a cigarette burning in an ashtray beside him, and a half-full glass of beer in front of him. The general appearance of the man, as well as the way he slurs every other word, indicates the half full beer was not his first. "Wow, Felton!...you brought a dead man with you!" The man's comment startles Patrick, and he gives Felton a suspicious scowl. "It's okay, Hartley" Felton assures him. "This is the man I brought you here to meet. This man is Curtis Flanagan...Dr. Curtis Flanagan." The man extends his arm toward Patrick to shake. "Good to see you again, Mr. Hartley." Patrick looks over at Felton with a puzzled look, then back over to the man. "See me again?...have we met before?" The man gives Felton a quick nod and Felton chimes in on cue. "He was your doctor, Mr. Hartley. Dr. Flanagan, although he doesn't look anything like it at this moment, is one of the most respected doctor's in the state. He is the head of Temple Neuroscience Center of Philadelphia...he..." Flanagan interrupts Felton mid-sentence. "*Was* one of the most respected doctors in the state. A lot has changed since then. Now, I'm just another guy on the run like you, Hartley." Patrick waits for him to continue but there is only silence, prompting him to ask the obvious question. "On the run from what?" Flanagan pauses to take a sip of beer before answering. "You mean on the run from whom, don't you Mr. Hartley?...the same people who are looking for you."

Patrick looks over at Felton yet again with an obvious look of confusion on his face. Felton address Dr. Flanagan..."tell him what he needs to know, Curtis." This prompts a brief chuckle from the doctor. "Oh, it's Curtis now? I didn't know we were on a first name basis, Benjamin." Felton raises his voice now, suddenly annoyed. "Are you going to help us or are you just going to waste out time?"

Flanagan laughs again before picking up the glass and taking another swig of beer. "No Ben, I'm not going to waste your time, none of us has much of that left now. Ok, here it is Hartley. As Dr. Felton already mentioned, I was the head of Temple University Neuroscience Center. My specialty there was treating patients with traumatic brain injury. We are considered the finest center in the state, and one of the finest in the nation for that matter, in treating such cases. You became my patient approximately three years ago. My expertise at the time involved working with a chemical called Citicoline to treat brain injury. I'll spare you the medical jargon but Citicoline is a naturally occurring compound in the human body. We have made a great deal of progress treating brain injury using a greatly enhanced form of this compound. Because of the vast extent of your injuries, I was placed in charge of your case. Unfortunately, my work was stopped just as it was getting started." Patrick shakes his head as if not understanding. "What do you mean it was stopped, stopped how?" Flanagan nods in the direction of Felton. "Stopped by Darden, Stadnik, and that guy standing next to you." Patrick looks over at Felton, who quickly breaks eye contact and stares down at the floor.

"I don't understand" Patrick says, "What do you mean?" Flanagan looks over at Felton, who is still staring at the floor, and shakes his head before continuing. "You were with us for approximately six days before you were suddenly transferred. I was told that you were being transferred to St, Joseph's Hospital. Now, nothing against St. Joe's but I was absolutely dumfounded by this. Why would they transfer you, considering your condition at the time, from the finest brain center in the state to there? When I raised this concern, I was told that I was ordered to oblige. I was told that your family had insisted on it because of religious reasons. It was explained to me that the family insisted you be transferred to a Catholic hospital. I asked if I could speak to your family, to make sure they knew the risks, but I was refused. The next day, I was told you never made it to St. Joe's. I was told you had passed away in an ambulance in route. Naturally, I was very suspicious. I investigated the matter on my own. As you can probably guess, I found out a lot more than I should have. I also found out that there have been other cases just like yours. In fact, there have been dozens. Patients with head trauma like yours, suddenly and inexplicably removed from care. I'm sure the good Dr. Felton over there could shed some light on that. What about it, Felton?"

Dr. Felton looks up and stares into the eyes of Flanagan before answering. "You give me far too much credit, Flanagan. You want to sit there and point the finger at me that's fine. The fact is though, gentleman, I'm no different than either of you. All three of us are defectors. We are now Darden's enemy. True, when this whole thing started I was part of it. Yes, I once believed in what I was doing. That was only in the beginning. I was kept in the dark just like you were. I was only told what I needed to know. I am not the enemy here…if anything I tried to stop it. The fact of the matter is that no amount of finger-pointing is going to change matters. Darden is out there…who knows how many there are or what they have planned. We are on the brink of disaster and we all know it. Darden is clearly trying to eliminate anyone who stands in his way. Anyone who has information about what he is up to…he will find them and eliminate them. If you don't believe me, just look at what happened to Dr. Stadnik." Hartley interrupts, "…or Anna Holloway. She obviously found out more than she should have, and it got her killed. We need to find out what she knew." Hartley steps closer to the two men and lowers his voice. "Listen, I'm past pointing the finger. Felton, I'd be dead back there on the expressway if you hadn't shown up…I get that. Whatever Darden and his zombies have in store for the rest of the world is the world's problem. All I'm interested in is my family. Here we are standing in this bar, three men with targets on our backs…just waiting. I can't afford to wait. If my family is out there, Darden is looking for them also. He is looking for them because he knows that is how he can get to me. You talk about defectors, Felton…I'm the biggest defector of all. Stadnik told me I was one of the first…one of the first guinea pigs in Darden's experiment. I'm the one he will come after first. What I need to know right now is if either of you have any information about my family. If not, we are just standing here wasting our time."

Flanagan stands up now, pushing himself away from the bar. He stares at Hartley and shakes his head. "I don't want to be the one to tell you this, Hartley, but someone has to. I don't think there is any way your family is still alive. After you left the hospital…after I learned you had passed away…I tried to connect with your wife. She had disappeared, Mr. Hartley, along with your daughter. I was told that no one has seen them since. Like I said, I don't want to be the one to tell you this, but I think you deserve to know. Although he tries his best to control them, Hartley can't prevent the tears from forming in his eyes. As much as he doesn't want to admit it to himself, he must deal with the possibility that Flanagan is right. "Maybe so Flanagan, maybe I'm too late. If that's the case…then there's no point of me living anyway. Before I'm dead though, I will find Owen Darden…I will find him, and he will pay for what he has done to me and my family." Felton sighs loudly and shakes his head. "You don't understand, Mr. Hartley. You don't understand the kind of people you are dealing with here. You need my help. You are right about one thing…Darden will come after you first. So, you need to be ready for him when he does. Follow me, it's time to go. The two men head toward the rear exit of the bar, leaving Dr. Flanagan standing there. Just as they are about to walk out the door, Flanagan calls out to them…"It's your funeral gentlemen." Flanagan then goes back to the bar, sits on the stool, and grabs his glass of beer. Before taking one last drink,

he holds the glass up, as if proposing a
toast…"here's to the end of the world…

17

The two men had agreed to take shifts. One would drive while the other one slept. Although barely past four o'clock in the afternoon, it had already been a long day. Felton had agreed to drive the first shift while Hartley napped. Considering how physically and emotionally drained Patrick was feeling, he had no desire to argue. He had fallen asleep quickly and it wasn't long before the dreams started. In much the same way as they had earlier, they came in fast moving frames. In one of the dreams, he was following an attractive woman down a city street. The street appeared to be the same one that Anna Holloway's office building was on. In fact, it appeared to be that the woman Patrick was following may have been Anna Holloway herself. The woman certainly matched the description that Stadnik had given him, blonde and attractive. She glanced around nervously and appeared to be aware that she was being followed. In another dream, Patrick was sitting in a crowded, dark room staring at a young couple at a table. The disturbing part of these dreams was not the content, but the overall mood of the dreams themselves. In both, he had felt as if he was in a trance of some kind. He sensed an uncontrollable anger. Not a willful anger…it was as if he was being driven in a direction he did not want to go but was powerless to stop. He awoke in fear, pulse racing, and beads of sweat on his forehead.

When Patrick had fully awakened, he also realized that the car was no longer in motion. Instead, Felton had pulled over to the side of the road. They were no longer on the highway, but on a paved single-lane road in a remote area. "How long was I sleeping?" Patrick asks. "You've been out about an hour… are you feeling alright Hartley?" Patrick rubs his eyes and shakes his head, trying to get his thoughts together. "Yeah, I'm fine…I was just dreaming." A look of concern comes over Felton's face. "Dreaming?...what kind of dream?" Lately, Felton had been asking these questions a lot, as if Patrick was his case study, and it was frankly becoming annoying. "I don't know, just a dream Felton. Where the hell are we anyway? Why did you leave the highway?" Felton motions out the window…"I thought you'd want to see this place…I thought it was a place you needed to see. This will be a good reminder to you of what we are up against. Back in the bar, you sounded like you were ready to take on Darden single-handedly. I need to know where your head is. Look out the window, do you know why we are here?" Patrick glances out the window. The car is parked next to a black wrought-iron gate with a sign reading "Cedar Ridge Cemetery." A rusty fence circles what is obviously a graveyard. "You brought me here to remind me that we both could be killed, right." Felton turns to Patrick and shakes his head slowly. "This isn't just any graveyard, Hartley. This is your graveyard. This is where your headstone is. Understand this…the one's that we are up against…Darden and those that are with him…they have the power to do anything they want. They were able to take control of you and make everyone believe you were dead. That's no small feat, Hartley. To pull something like that off, you need resources and power that goes way beyond Darden himself. This is what we're up against, Hartley. Absolute power...unlike anything we've seen before. Do you understand that?" Patrick stares at the cemetery sign, a million thoughts swimming in his head. "Yes, I understand what we are up against. I also know that I am not like you or Stadnik. I am just some ordinary guy who has been thrown in the middle of this nightmare. I know you feel responsible for what has happened to me and maybe you are. Now you don't want my blood on your hands. I will tell you this, Felton. I know what my chances are...one man against god knows how many out there. I am willing to take that chance because it's all I have left. I refuse to sit around and be a victim anymore." Felton turns back around in the driver's seat and starts the car. "Ok Hartley let's go...and one more thing...It's not just you against them. I'm going with you. If we are going to die, we are going to die together. I'm not letting my partner die in vain. I owe that much to Dr. Stadnik. If you are going to bring Darden down, I'm going to bring him down with you."

Felton puts the car into drive and begins to pull back out onto the road. "Wait!" Patrick shouts suddenly. "I need to see it." Felton turns to Patrick with a puzzled look on his face. "Need to see what?" Patrick motions in the direction beyond the black gate. "I need to see the grave. Don't ask me why, I just need to see it." Felton shakes his head. "Now you're the one wasting time, Hartley. What do you need to see it for?... why would you want to?" Before he even attempts to answer, Patrick is already opening the passenger door and stepping out of the car. "Alright, fine Hartley...at least take the gun." Felton reached under the passenger seat and grabs the gun from where Patrick had placed it. "Here, take this and follow me." Felton hands Patrick the gun and the two men head off in the direction of the graveyard. There is nothing at all different about this grave. It is your typical headstone..

PATRICK M. HARTLEY

1980-2015

BELOVED HUSBAND AND FATHER

To anyone passing through the cemetery, it is just one of dozens of headstones. To Patrick, of course, nothing on earth could look more bizarre. A tidal wave of emotions pass through him as he stares at the stone. First, a feeling of rage and an indescribable thirst for revenge. Then, a feeling of loss and despair. Something else that is odd about the gravesite jumps out at him. Something that he then points out to Felton. "Fresh flowers" Patrick says, pointed to a bouquet of fresh-looking purple and gold lilies. "Yeah, I saw that" Felton says. "Well?" Patrick continues, "Don't you think that's a little odd? Someone must have been here recently. But who? Don't you think that could be some sort of sign?" Felton pauses, then looks over at Patrick and shrugs. "I know what you're getting at, Hartley. You want to believe that your wife and kid were here. You want to believe that they are trying to leave you some message." Patrick looks over at Felton with a hint of a smile on his face. "You said that, Felton, I didn't. But how do you know it wasn't them? I could have been them." Felton is having none of it. "Or, it could have been anyone, Hartley. People come to graves sometimes. Sometimes they even leave flowers. Sorry, but I'm not buying it. You had to have had some friends. Someone besides your family. Like I said, it could have been anyone." Patrick continues to stare down at the gravesite and the bouquet of flowers. "Yeah, I know you're right…it's just…it's just a feeling I have…I can't explain it. Maybe I'm crazy…I'm pretty sure I am. To you they are just flowers but to me it's a sign." The two men stand in silence for another moment, then Felton taps Patrick on the shoulder. "Come on, we need to go." Just as Patrick glances back over at Felton, he hears a loud popping noise above his right shoulder. Felton looks over at Patrick with his eyes wide and his mouth open, as if in awe. Felton then makes a loud grunting noise and falls to his knees. As Patrick tries to process what is happening, he sees the blood.

It appears that the bullet has penetrated the center of Felton's back, just below the bottom of his neck. "Felton!...Oh Christ! Patrick calls out. Felton falls all the way to the ground and is lying face-down. Patrick quickly rolls him over. One look at the man's face tells Patrick all he needs to know. Felton is in deep trouble. His eyes are now completely closed, and his breathing is labored. There is a small, gurgling sound emanating from his chest with each heavy breath. "Oh god, Felton…hang on…just hang on!" Patrick looks up and gazes around hopelessly. Just then, he sees a man in dark clothing running across the front entrance of the graveyard, just on the other side of the iron gate. Although he doesn't want to leave Felton in this condition, he knows he must go after him. Patrick had only taken the gun to appease Felton and he had no intention of ever using it. Now, the thought occurs to him that he probably has no idea how to use it. There is no time to debate this in his mind. With weapon in hand, he sprints toward the front entrance of the cemetery.

When he arrives at the front of the cemetery, he stops briefly by the car and debates whether to pursue the man by foot or by car. His mind is now spinning in a thousand different directions. He has no idea which direction the man has gone. How will he ever find him? Just then, another loud popping sound. This time the sound comes from directly behind him. For a brief millisecond, Patrick expects to feel a huge rush of pain and collapse himself. He then realizes the bullet has missed him, evidenced by the shattering of glass from the car in front of him. Patrick quickly spins around and drops to one knee. He sees the shooter now, less than fifty yards in front of him and crouched down in the shrubbery. The shooter fires again, this time the bullet strikes the door of the car less than six inches from where Patrick is kneeling. Patrick Hartley would later ponder the events of the next three seconds with the sense that these were the strangest events of all. All in one motion…without even realizing that he knew how…Patrick releases the safety from the weapon, points the gun, and fires. For that one instant, there is feeling that control of his body has been seized by some unknown force. He feels as though time has slowed…as if he is dreaming in slow motion. He can almost follow the path of the bullet as it exits the chamber…flies toward the unknown assailant…through the shrubbery…striking the man directly in his chest. Without hesitation, Patrick climbs to his feet and sprints toward the man, who is now sprawled on his back. Patrick stands over him, finally getting a good look at the assailant. He looks very young, perhaps no more than twenty. He has light skin and blonde hair. Lying on the ground, he looks like nothing more than a little boy. Patrick also sees the large amount of blood coming from the wound in his chest. The young man is still alive and is attempting to speak. He looks up at Patrick and moves his lips as if trying to say something. Patrick looks down at him and asks, "who are you?...who sent you?" The young man's breaths become increasingly shallow and farther apart. He looks up one last time at Patrick, a look of desperation on his face. "Please make it stop…please make it go away…the pain...the itching...please make it go away." His breathing becomes even more shallow and increasingly scattered...then stops altogether. Patrick watched the young man die with his eyes wide open. In his expression, Patrick can almost detect a look of relief on his face...he is finally at peace.

Patrick Hartley has returned to the cemetery now, and stares down at the body of Dr. Benjamin Felton. Felton also has a peaceful look on his face, as if he has come to the end of a long journey. Patrick kneels beside him, breaks down, and begins to sob. He cries for his wife and child, for Anna Holloway, for Stadnik, and for Felton. He even cries for the young man lying in the bushes outside the cemetery. Most of all, he cries because of the hopelessness of it all. Patrick stares down at Felton one last time. He takes one more look at the peaceful expression on his face, suddenly longing for peace himself. These emotions seem to briefly take control of him as he glances over his gravesite. Patrick lifts the gun to the side of his own head, contemplating putting an end to all the hopelessness. Only one thing stops him...the purple and gold lilies.

18

Dr. Curtis Flanagan slowly twirls the nearly empty beer glass on the bar, swirling the small bit of liquid inside. He remains in the same spot where he has spent nearly the entire day. Attempts at drowning his problems in Guinness have resulted only in a dull headache and a terrible taste in his mouth. The earlier visit from Felton and Hartley, along with the discussion of Darden and all that has happened, has returned him to that dark place he tries so hard to escape from. He is fully aware that he is a target...a defector of Darden, as Felton put it. How did it all go so wrong? How did he go from Dr. Flanagan, Head of Neuroscience at Temple University Hospital, to this? He was a great doctor who loved what he did, helping to cure illness and save lives. Every day, he would walk past the sign at the hospital entrance...the sign that displayed the facility motto. Right after those words... health and wellness...caring and compassion. He believed in those words...he used to believe in them anyway. It was caring and compassion that landed him here. Because he was unable to accept the explanation of Hartley's transfer from Temple's Trauma Center to St. Joe's...because he had to investigate...because he cared. Finally, it might be his caring and compassion that proves to be the death of him...literally.

Curtis has chosen to isolate himself, deciding to hide himself away from the world in this lonely, old Irish bar. His brother-in-law Mitch inherited the place two years ago. He began remodeling six months after that and it still has not opened to the public. Inflated repair costs, along with a general poor sense of planning have contributed to the delays. Curtis' brother-in-law is known around town as somewhat of a shady character, using the bar mostly to entertain the equally shady "business associates" he deals with. Mitch has also done time in jail, and twice Curtis has received late night phone calls from his brother-in-law asking to be bailed out. "Please

Curtis, your sister will kill me if I call her." Suffice it to say, Mitch hasn't been a hit with the family since Curtis' sister Haley first started bringing him around. Consequently, his presence at family functions creates constant grief and turmoil. Despite this, Curtis has grown very fond of him. Despite his faults, Mitch is a kind-hearted guy and loyal friend. It also doesn't hurt that he keeps the Guinness flowing from the tap at no charge. In return, Curtis promises to turn a blind eye to some of his "extracurricular activities." At this moment, Curtis is beginning to wonder if more trouble hasn't found his brother-in-law. He was due back hours ago, although reliability has never been one of his strong suits. Curtis has no intention of setting out to find him just yet. Mitch, somewhat of a problem gambler, can usually be found either at a track or an offsite betting location somewhere in the area. If he is having a good night picking horses, he has been known to disappear for hours at a time…something that doesn't sit too well with his wife. He also has been known to try to lore Curtis into joining him, but he is never successful. For one, Curtis has never been a gambler. He has never understood the fascination of watching horses run around on a track. Another reason is a

secret fear that Curtis has, one that he shares with
no one…a fear of the night. As a young doctor,
Curtis Flanagan interned as an emergency room
physician. As any intern in the ER will tell you, the
nighttime hours are the busiest. Drunk driving
accidents, shootings, muggings, stabbings…all
these things occur much more frequently at night.
The everyday tragedies and human suffering that
he has seen in his job have taken a toll on him.
They have made him fearful of his own well-being
and acutely aware of his own mortality. He has
fallen into a pattern that many doctors fall into. He
spends far too many hours indulging in alcohol,
has had very few meaningful relationships, and
involves himself in his patients' lives much more
than he should.

Curtis gets up from the stool and walks
around the bar to pour one last drink. He looks up
at the clock which now reads 10:05pm. Shaking his
head as he pours the beer, he mutters out loud,
"where the hell are you, Mitch?" Almost
immediately, as if in answer to his question, the
phone behind the bar begins to ring. Curtis walks
over to the phone and picks it up. "This better be
good Mitch, what's the excuse this
time?…Mitch?…Mitch, are you there?" At first,

Curtis hears nothing on the other end of the line but rapid breathing. Soon, he begins to hear some muffled conversation in the background. He hears someone say, "answer him…answer him now." Curtis brings his free hand up to cover his other ear, trying to hear better. "Mitch, is that you?...what's going on?" Finally, his brother-in-law speaks. "Curtis, listen to me and don't say anything…I'm in trouble here." Curtis feels his heart pounding. "Oh shit, what now Mitch…what did you do this time?" He hears more rustling in the phone. "Shut up Curtis!...just shut up and listen!...I can't talk for very long…I can't explain right now…you've got to come to where I am. There are some people here, Curtis. There are some people here and I don't know them. You have to come here, Curtis…you have to come here or they're going to kill me!" In his panic, Curtis knocks the beer glass from the bar and is startled by the sound of the glass shattering on the floor. "Who is with you, Mitch?...what do they want?" There is a pause now and Curtis hears muffled conversation. It sounds as though someone has their hand over the phone and there is arguing in the background. Finally, Mitch returns to the phone. "Curtis, I'm going to give you an address.

You need to leave right now and come by yourself. Don't call the police…don't call anyone or we're both dead." A rush of fear passes through Curtis as he fumbles for pen and paper. "Okay, give me the address." He quickly scribbles it down then says, "Okay Mitch, I've got it." He hears the panic in his brother-in-law's voice… "Hurry Curtis and remember…no police and come alone." He hears some more fumbling around on the other end of the phone and the line goes dead.

He had grabbed the car keys to his silver Audi and run out the door without any regard for his fear of the night. It wasn't until he was halfway to the address Mitch had given him that reality set in.. Now, given more time to think about his situation, the cold hand of fear was beginning to tap him hard on the shoulder. In his rush to get to his brother-in-law, he had not stopped to think about what he was headed into . He was going there alone and unarmed. He had no idea what kind of trouble Mitch had found but, judging by his reaction on the phone, it was likely something terrifying. Curtis knows that Mitch is not one to scare easily. He knew his brother-in-law had run into trouble before and could handle himself in a confrontation. Still, he had sounded so helpless on the phone…as if Curtis had been talking to a frightened child. He had no idea who or what had Mitch so terrified, but he had a good guess….Darden.

Curtis is not at all familiar with the address Mitch has given him. He is, however, very familiar with the area. The section that the street is on is a section of Philadelphia that sends a lot of business the hospital's way. It is the type of place you wouldn't want to drive past on a bet…an area of Philly you might happen upon if you were lost…and you would pray your car would not break down. He turns off Washington Boulevard and onto Jefferson. Jefferson is a dark street, despite the many light posts on either side of the road. The street is dark because the lights have been shot out by street thugs and dealers. These are not people you see when you are passing but they see you. They hide in the shadows and wait for a car to slow down. Curtis wonders how he is being judged right now…as a junky looking for a score…or a lost traveler who is about to be carjacked. He tries his best to remove these thoughts from his mind as he turns off Jefferson and onto Suffix. He sees the address that he is looking for on

Suffix…138. The number is written on a mailbox but there is no house on the road…only a gravel driveway that leads down into darkness. Curtis sits in the car for a moment and contemplates his next move. Finally, with great hesitation, he turns the car onto the gravel. "Mitch, you owe me for this one."

He sees that there is small house at the bottom of the driveway. The house is completely dark inside and looks abandoned. Curtis nearly decides to turn the car around when he notices a vehicle parked along the side of the house. He immediately recognizes the rusty, red Ford Pickup…Mitch's truck. He feels his stomach drop now as a feeling of dread comes over him. He parks the Audi behind his brother-in-law's truck and waits. What finally catches his eye is the light on the porch. Someone inside the house blinks the porch light on and then off again. Seconds later, the same pattern repeats. Curtis realizes that this is a signal for him to walk toward to the house. Obviously, he is far from anxious to do this. His hands shake almost uncontrollably as he puts the vehicle in park and removes the keys from the ignition. The twenty or so paces to the front door feel to Curtis like a death march…complete with a bass drum that is his thumping heart. He finally arrives at the front door of the house and pauses again. Suddenly, the door creaks open…pulled by someone from inside.

Despite his ever-growing fear of what waits for him in the darkness, Curtis forces himself to take one small step forward, then another. His feet feel like two lead weights as he crosses the threshold and enters the dark hallway. He squints his eyes, trying to adjust his vision to the darkness. At first, he sees and hears no one. Finally, he can stand the terror of the unknown no longer. He calls out now, although sound barely escapes from his lips. "Mitch…are you there?" His first attempt goes unanswered. "Mitch…answer me…are you there?" This time, a voice answers him. The voice that answers does not belong to Mitch, however. This voice is much deeper…too deep…as if someone is trying to disguise their true voice. "Stand right where you are, and don't even think about coming closer. Right now, there are two guns pointed at your head. You might not be able to see them but, believe me, they are there." Curtis stands in a frozen position and drops his arms to his side. The voice continues, "I hope you've come alone, and for your sake, I hope you didn't call the police." Curtis stares into the darkness, trying to focus on what is ahead of him. "Who are you?...what do you want?...where's Mitch?" The deep voice answers…"we will get to that, Dr. Flanagan. If you play your cards right, you and your worthless brother-in-law might even make it out of here alive. That will be up to you, of course. As for who I am, let's just say I am someone who doesn't like to lose. Let's just say I am someone who doesn't like it when someone tries to make me lose. Let's also say that you have been quite bothersome, Dr. Flanagan. People like you need to learn to mind your own business and know your place in the world. You seem to have a hard time doing that, Dr. Flanagan. With this comment, Curtis is almost certain he knows who he is talking to. "Darden, it's you isn't it?" Now Curtis hears laughter from the man. "Curtis Flanagan, always the inquisitive doctor. I think you need to be less worried about who I am and more worried about survival. You see, Dr. Flanagan, I intend to survive…do you?" The voice pauses, as if waiting for Curtis to answer. "I want to know what you've done with Mitch…where is he?...what have you done to him?" The voice grows louder now and more impatient. "I think you should be more worried about what I am going to do to you!"

Curtis feels himself beginning to unravel. He feels like he is slipping away into a dark and cold place. As a doctor, he is familiar with the early signs of shock. He begins to recognize the symptoms within himself which frightens him. Also familiar with techniques of relaxation, Curtis tries to steady himself and focus on his breathing. There is no sound for the next several seconds, as if they are in the middle of a chess match, waiting for the other to make the next move. Finally it is Curtis who breaks the silence. "What do you want from me?" The man chuckles again, an evil chuckle, then begins to answer. "Think back to when you were a child, Dr. Flanagan….before you put on that white medical coat of yours and started playing god. Did you ever play with puzzles? I'm sure you did. Anyway, imagine you have spent hours, weeks, and years putting together the grandest puzzle ever constructed. Now, imagine you are almost finished with this amazing puzzle when you find that there are just a few pieces missing. You see the empty spaces where the pieces are supposed to fit, but they are nowhere to be found. Unfortunately, that's where I am Dr. Flanagan. I had the pieces all in place but now some are missing. You are going to help me get those pieces back. Do you understand?"

Curtis stands there in silence, his mind busy trying to make sense of the strange analogy. "I don't understand what you mean." Once again, a chuckle. "Oh, but I think you do understand. You and I are not so different, Dr. Flanagan. People like you and me are always striving to change the world. But you sir, have become a most bothersome person to me. You have conspired to change the outcome of my plan. I can't accept that, Dr. Flanagan. For this reason, you will help me finish what I started. Once these pieces have been recovered…and my puzzle is finally completed…the world will change forever." Curtis' head feels like it is spinning as he tries to keep up with what is being said. No matter how hard he tries, he is confused as ever. "Whatever it is you are planning to do, what makes you think I can help you? What are these pieces that you are talking about?" The man pauses for a few seconds before continuing. "I'm a little disappointed that you don't know, Dr. Flanagan. After all, he was your patient. I thought you cared about your patients." Finally, Curtis begins to understand. "You are talking about Hartley?" What makes you think I can get him back for you?" Curtis can sense the man becoming increasingly impatient. "Because he will trust you…because he has no one left. You see, Dr. Flanagan, it seems as though Hartley teamed up with an ex-colleague of mine…a certain Dr. Benjamin Felton. Earlier today, we located them not far from here. Hartley got away but Felton wasn't so lucky. When we searched Felton's body, we also discovered his phone missing. We assume that Hartley must have taken it. So that leads us back to where we are now. Hartley is out there, and he is alone. He needs someone to trust. That's where you come in, Dr. Flanagan. It's time to make a choice…a choice for you and Mitch…live or die. Just then, Curtis hears a loud clap of thunder behind him. For a second, he mistakes the noise for a gun shot. An image passes through his mind…an image of himself lying in a pool of his own blood. "Ok Darden, you win…I'll do it."

19

The rain pounds on the windshield of the Dodge Caravan as Beverly Holloway tries desperately to focus on the road in front of her. The wipers swish back and forth rhythmically but are unable to keep up with the onslaught of water brought on by the late-summer thunderstorm. Beverly occasionally glances into the rearview mirror which she has tilted forward in order to keep her eyes on the sleeping child in the back seat. She has no idea where they are headed, she only knows that they need to leave the house in King of

Prussia far behind. She has a strong sense that they are fleeing something more than just the two intruders who entered the house earlier in the evening. She flashes back to the ominous warning from the man with the balloons…"you need to take her and leave…leave before they find you." The warning she had foolishly tried to brush aside…to disregard as a misunderstanding. Considering the events which would unfold just hours later, she is sure now that the child is not safe…that neither of them is safe. Someone has come for them…someone wishes to harm them…maybe the same people who took Anna from her.

She replays the events of the break-in over and over in her mind. The mere thought of what could have happened causes her to shiver in terror. Fortunately, the two men had been frightened off by a vehicle pulling up to the curb outside. Maybe, the men had figured someone had returned home. Maybe they thought the police had come. The noise outside turned out to be Larry Mitchell, her neighbor coming home from work and parking his van on the side of the street. As soon as she heard the two men leave out the back door, she had run over to the Mitchell's, carrying the child in her arms. Larry, upon being told of the break-in, immediately wanted to phone the police. Just as he was starting to dial the phone, something told Beverly to stop him. An unexplainable feeling had come over her, a feeling that calling the police would not be the right thing to do. As if a voice had whispered in her ear…as if she was being guided by someone…as if Anna was talking to her from beyond. Bev has always heard that the bond between mother and daughter is so strong that the connection can never be broken…even by death. She now believes in this connection more than ever before. She knows it would sound unbelievable to some. She would sound just like anyone else who doesn't want to believe that their loved one is really gone. Beverly does believe that Frank and Anna are still with her, and the dead never really leave us. She believes that they still exist among us, albeit in a different kind of reality. Their souls want to help those that they love…see them through the dark times…guide them back into the light. She is sure that Frank and Anna are with them and will help keep them safe.

The storm is unrelenting, dumping buckets of rain on the expressway. Flashes of lightning illuminate the nighttime sky, followed by crashes of loud thunder. The little girl in the backseat remains asleep, oblivious to the loud booms and flashes of light happening around her. Bev is following behind an eighteen-wheeler down the highway, staying close enough to the truck's bumper to block some of the driving rain, yet far enough to stop suddenly if necessary. She thinks back to a time years ago, before Anna was born, when Bev and Frank got caught in a vicious snowstorm returning from a funeral in Indiana. This was back in the time of the CB Radio craze. It seemed that every adult male had one in their vehicle at the time. They created fancy names, or handles, for themselves. Men trying to pass themselves off as truckers while carting their families around in a station wagon. Bev's husband, Frank Holloway, was also caught up in this craze. He outfitted himself with a fancy handle, "Midnight Cowboy" and he loved to tune his Cobra CB Radio to channel 19…the trucker's channel. Beverly would laugh and roll her eyes as Frank would chat it up with truckers…"10-4 good buddy, what's your twenty?" It was on that trip from Indiana though, where Bev developed a newfound respect for the CB Radio and truckers in general. While trying to drive through the fierce snowstorm, Frank began conversing with a trucker who was just ahead of them. The snowstorm had become absolutely blinding, the road becoming increasingly treacherous. If it hadn't been for this truck driver, a nice man from Ohio with the handle "Road Dog" they may never have made it home that night. The trucker instructed Frank to stay behind him and maintain a steady speed. Road Dog guided them all the way through the snowstorm that night and may have very well saved their lives. Although they never saw him again, Frank and Beverly never forgot that trucker, a most unlikely guardian angel. Ever since that day, Bev has always made it a habit to locate a trucker on the road during bad weather. She always tries to stay right behind them if possible. Truckers know the road and they will guide you to safety. Right now, Beverly is counting on guidance from the trucker…as well as Frank and Anna…her other guardian angels.

Bev is startled by the voice of the little girl behind her… "where are we going?" Beverly tries to maintain her focus on the road while attempting to reassure the young girl. "It's alright sweetie, I'm going to find us a safe place for the night." The child remains silent for a moment before asking, "are the bad people going to get us?" Beverly glances into the rearview mirror and sees the frightened eyes of the young girl. "Listen to me carefully. I am not going to let anything happen to you, not today and not ever. I am with you and you are safe, do you understand me?" The child nods her head and answers quietly, "yes ma'am." The sound of her poor little voice is almost enough to make Bev cry. Then the little girl says something Beverly was half expecting but was hoping she wouldn't hear at this moment. "Ma'am, I have to go to the bathroom." Again, Bev looks in the rearview mirror. "Honey, are you absolutely sure you have to go? Can't you wait just a little longer?" Although hoping for a different answer, Beverly is not surprised when the little girl replies, "no ma'am." Beverly chooses the next exit for the town of Hammonton, New Jersey. The big billboard off the exit proclaims the town as the blueberry capital of the world. Right now, Beverly has no interest in visiting the town. The thought of trading the warmth and safety of the vehicle for the harsh elements outside seems less than inviting. Still, she reassures the child. "Just hang on a bit longer, we are going to find a nice, safe place to go into...don't worry." Beverly drives a bit farther and finally does find a suitable place. She pulls into a convenience store that appears to be relatively clean. The large, spinning sign in the parking lot displays a clever name for the store...The Red, White, and Blueberry Shop, an obvious reference to the town's pride and joy. "Alright little one, we need to run in and run back out, okay?" It's storming badly out there. Are you ready...on a count of three...one...two...three...let's go!!" They run holding hands into the store, as fast as their legs will carry them.

While Beverly waits for the little girl outside the door of the bathroom, she occupies her time by reading a brochure from a rack in the back of the store. The brochure is a visitor's guide to the town of Hammonton. With a population of 13,000, Hammonton is indeed famous for its blueberries. They are apparently considered the freshest, sweetest blueberries to be found. Every year, the town also hosts a famous Blueberry Festival. The brochure boasts that many famous people have attended the festival, including former president Ronald Reagan. Bev goes about her reading until the bathroom door opens and the little girl emerges. "You're all set now?" The little girl nods her head. "Okay then, let's go." She leads the child by the hand toward the front of the store. Another customer is leaving at the same time, a rugged looking young man with a dirty flannel shirt, faded blue jeans, and a weathered ball cap. He holds the door open for them and begins to initiate a conversation with Beverly. "I saw you over there looking at the brochure. Are you staying around here? This is a great little town, you know?. Wait until you try the blueberries. The storm has slowed now to no more than a drizzle. Beverly also notices a damp, heaviness to the night air. She also notices that she is becoming increasingly anxious, as if something is telling her to leave as quickly as possible. "The town seems lovely, and I'm sure the blueberries are delectable. Unfortunately though, we're just passing through." The man continues to follow them. "Well, you should really try to get back here sometime. There's no other place I'd rather be than Hammonton." Beverly grips the child's hand tighter and leads her toward their vehicle. "Perhaps someday we will return, good night now." The man tips his cap to them and starts to walk in the direction of a white tow truck parked across the lot. He turns around one more time and waves in their direction. "You two be safe now, it's dangerous out there."

The tow truck driver's warning soon turned into something more of a prophecy. Just when she thought the storm had subsided, a second outburst of weather erupts just as they are pulling out of the parking lot. This second storm brings torrential downpours and heavy winds. The rain appears to be moving sideways now in blinding sheets. Beverly moves forward in the driver's seat and tries her best to focus on what's in front of her. As each second passes, it becomes increasingly difficult to see anything through the deluge of water hammering the windshield. She has obviously missed a turn and is on a side street now somewhere in Hammonton. Amazingly, the young girl in the back seat remains oblivious to all of this. She had fallen back to sleep right after Bev had pulled out of the store parking lot. For the first time, true fear takes hold of Beverly. True, she had been afraid at the time of the break-in. At that moment though, she hardly had time to be truly frightened. She had an immediate sense of purpose at that moment…to protect the child. Adrenalin had taken over and quelled her fears. Now, with the child sleeping in the backseat, and the only sound around her the driving rain, she feels an eerie presence of fear so close to her…as if it is sitting in the passenger seat right next to her.

Reluctantly, Beverly decides that her only recourse is to pull the vehicle over and wait for the downpour to pass. Carefully, she eases the Dodge Caravan onto the shoulder of the side street and puts the vehicle in park. She glances at the child still sound asleep in the backseat, then looks out the windows on either side. From what she can see through the smeared, rain-soaked glass, there is nothing around them. She curses at herself for not remembering to grab her cell phone. Once again, she is reminded of Anna who insisted that she purchase one. Anna always feared that Beverly would be somewhere late at night needing help. "What would you do then, mom?" Bev would always say to Anna that she thought the idea was silly…"but Anna, I'm never out late at night." Eventually, knowing Bev would never purchase one herself, Anna got her mother a cell phone. The problem was, Beverly hardly ever carried it. Something that always drove Anna nuts. Bev considers herself, as Anna calls it, technically challenged. She has no desire to be part of the world of cell phones and high-speed everything. Just the same, at this moment, she wishes she had listened to her daughter and carried the phone. Now, all she can do is sit and wait for the storm to subside.

Beverly leans her head back on the headrest. For the first time since Anna's memorial service, she cries. She cries not just because of sadness, but also because of the fear and helplessness she feels at this moment. Her intention is only to help this poor, innocent child…to protect her from all that is dangerous in the world. Now, sitting in the parked SUV and unable to move, she realizes that she is powerless to protect her. Just when all seems lost and the darkness outside seems to be closing in, she sees lights approaching behind her. At first, a rush of relief passes through her…as if the weight of the world has been lifted from her shoulders. Slowly, however, that warm rush of relief is replaced by a certain indescribable coldness. The vehicle approaching them has lights, maybe a police car. Until it is just a few feet away does Beverly realize exactly what it is. Soon, she can see the vehicle more clearly and realizes it is not a police car but a tow truck. Two men quickly exit the truck. One of the men she immediately recognizes as the same one from the convenience store. Before she can react, the man opens the driver's side door of the SUV, reaches for her keys, and yanks them out of the ignition. Frozen in fear,

Beverly looks at the man who is staring down at her smiling. "Mrs. Holloway, I knew we'd meet again…but not this soon."

20

Dr. Curtis Flanagan had been blindfolded and led down a rear staircase of the house on Suffix with a gun held to his back. His captures had warned him against making any sudden movements or any kind of sound. Although deprived of sight, he was able to detect that he wasn't the only prisoner being led down the stairs. Listening carefully, he was able to hear the breathing sounds and footsteps of one person behind him and two more ahead of him. The person behind him, judging by the cold metal of a gun pressed against his back, was obviously one of his captures. The other two, he assumed, were also hostages. One, he figured, was probably his brother-in-law Mitch. He had no idea who the other one might be. Listening to the footsteps and breathing of the other person made Curtis think that it may be a female. Although he had no way of confirming if he was correct, this was at least his suspicion. With each step, he tried to calm himself. He tried his best not to think about the gun pointed to his back and what was in store for him. He reminded himself that, for now at least, his life would be spared. After all, he thought, Darden needed him. He was the link to Patrick Hartley and that's who Darden really wanted. All he could do now is cooperate and do as he was told, even if that meant helping Darden get to Hartley. Although he had nothing against Patrick Hartley, his own family was involved now. Mitch's life was at stake, and therefore Curtis' sister's life. He couldn't bear the thought of his sister finding out that her husband was dead. He didn't think that she would be able to cope with such a tragedy. Furthermore, Curtis would never be able to live with himself knowing that he had a chance to save Mitch's life and failed. He would sooner die himself than allow that to happen.

Once they had reached the bottom of the

stairs, Curtis could tell by the cold dampness of the air and the musty smell that they were in a basement. This didn't seem like any ordinary basement however. It had obviously been reconstructed so that it contained several separate rooms. He knew this because of the sound of the doors opening and closing, and by the voices of their captures. When they first paused at the bottom of the stairs, the man with the gun ordered them to freeze and remain quiet. He then heard the man walk over to one of the hostages and say, "you...come with me." Curtis then heard footsteps as one of the hostages was led into a room on his left. After hearing the door close and lock, the man returned for the second hostage. "Now you...let's go." He led the second hostage to a room on Curtis' right. Finally, the man returned for Curtis. He was led further down the basement hallway where he heard a third door open. He was led inside another room and violently shoved forward. As he was pushed, Curtis lost his footing and fell to his knees, crashing down on a cold, hard floor. "Remember, we are right outside the door. Yell out, and you're dead." He then heard the door slam and lock.

Curtis stands and removes the blindfold. He is not able to see much more than he could with the blindfold on. All he can see is that he is in a small, dark room with four concrete walls with a bare, concrete floor beneath his feet. The door in front of him seems to be made of solid steel. He presses an ear to it and listens intently but can't hear a sound. He then runs his hands along each of the rough walls, searching for anything resembling an escape route. Finding nothing but solid cement, Curtis begins to feel like an animal trapped in a cage. He spends the next several minutes pacing back and forth, resembling a lion in a den. Finally, he collapses to the floor in frustration, places his hands over his face, and begins to sob. The darkness and isolation proves too much for him, the feeling of hopelessness growing more pronounced by the second. Why hasn't Darden come for him?...why hasn't he been asked to make the phone call to Hartley? He also wonders about Mitch and whether his brother-in-law is even still alive. Curtis had assumed that Mitch was one of the other hostages being led downstairs, but he has no proof of this. What if Mitch had never been in the house in the first place?...what if he was already dead? Just when it seemed he could stand the torment of the unknown no longer, he hears the steel door beginning to unlock. As this is happening, he also hears a voice.

"Step away from the door, Dr. Flanagan, and stand with your back to the far wall…we are coming in. Through the darkness, Curtis sees the figures of two men. One of them appears to be holding something he assumes to be a gun. "Don't move from where you are. If you take one step closer, you're dead." The man that he is speaking with now is the same person who spoke to him upstairs…Darden. "Well, Dr. Flanagan, it seems now we have some difficult decisions to make…" Curtis, now at the end of his rope, has no intention of remaining quiet during another of Darden's tirades. "Listen Darden, I already said I would do what you want me to do. We both know that Hartley is the one you really want. You want me to call him…fine, I'll call him. First, I want you to let Mitch go. He has nothing to do with this. This is between you and me. Again, Darden responds with a maniacal laugh. "Glad to see you have this all figured out, Dr. Flanagan…such a great doctor you are. You have made the diagnosis and written me out the prescription. Unfortunately, I'm not one of your patients and you don't make the orders here. Although we are similar, Dr. Flanagan, we are not the same. For one thing, I'm a far less compassionate man than you are. Although I'm impressed with the loyalty you've shown to your worthless brother-in-law, I'm also a man who doesn't like to be interrupted. If I were you, I wouldn't let it happen again." Darden pauses deliberately now, as if daring Curtis to speak before continuing. "As I started to say before I was rudely interrupted, we have some difficult decisions to make. Originally, I intended to use you to get to Hartley…but there has been a change of plans."

Curtis stands in silence, trying to make sense of the words being spoken. Darden pauses, as if wanting to build suspense before continuing. "If you recall our conversation upstairs, I made mention of some certain missing puzzle pieces. As you correctly surmised, Patrick Hartley is one of those missing pieces. He is not the only missing piece, however. As luck would have it, I've been notified that some other missing pieces of the puzzle have been found, just this evening. This is very good news for us and brings us that much closer to eliminating any holes in our plan. Unfortunately, this is not such good news for you and Mitch. You see, the individuals we found tonight carry a much a greater hope of being able to help us reel in Hartley. Sorry to say, Dr. Flanagan, but your services won't be needed after all." This Curtis understands immediately, and the fear grips him tightly. "What are you talking about, Darden, we had a deal. You said if I helped you, Mitch and I would walk out of here. " Darden takes a step closer to Curtis but remains far enough away to be out of arm's reach. "That's not very realistic, is it Dr. Flanagan. You see, we are at a crucial juncture right now. I have worked too hard for too long to let anything get in the way of my plan. The fact is that you mean very little to me. Your brother-in-law means even less to me. Your problem is that you have gotten in the way. But then again, that's always been your problem since the beginning. You see, the events that are on the horizon will change the world as we know it. When you are talking about a plan as ambitious as this, you don't leave anything to chance."

Curtis is beginning to feel light-headed and feels like he may pass out. He steadies himself against the concrete wall to keep from falling. "What is it, Darden?...what is it that you are planning to do?" The question seems to amuse Darden as he begins to answer with a laugh.

"Again, the curious doctor…right up to the end. Let me just answer you by saying that one of the most basic desires of every great man is to have a legacy…something they are remembered for. I deserve to be remembered, Dr. Flanagan. I am the creator of what will be remembered as the most important scientific discovery of our time…a discovery that will change the world as we know it. For such a discovery, one should be worshipped and revered. Instead, I was pushed aside and silenced. I was disregarded while others tried to pass my work off as their own. This result, Dr. Flanagan, is unacceptable to me. I will have my legacy…I demand it…and soon, the whole world will have no choice but to see it." This time Darden pauses, inviting Curtis to respond. "So for this?" Curtis asks…"this legacy you're talking about…you are willing to sell your soul?…to turn your back on your country?…on humanity?" Darden takes a step back from Curtis and motions for the man with him to do the same. He raises his voice, obviously infuriated by the questions. "Are you talking about patriotism, Dr. Flanagan? Are you talking about loyalty? These things mean absolutely nothing to me, and they shouldn't mean anything to you. Loyalty and patriotism are dead!...this country is dead!...it's all about greed and money now. That's all that's left! Now, if you will excuse me, Dr. Flanagan, I need to go greet some very special guests. Don't worry, we will be returning for you soon enough." Darden and the man leave the room, slamming and locking the door behind them.

21

Patrick Hartley had concluded his terrible evening by driving the tan Lexus several miles from the graveyard, finding a secluded spot to park the vehicle, and forcing himself to sleep for a few hours. Strangely, despite the violence which occurred there, he was reluctant to leave the graveyard. He felt this way for two reasons. One had to do with the lilies at his grave marker. He still felt, despite the doubts that Felton had expressed, that the flowers symbolized something he just couldn't put his finger on. He wasn't buying the fact that the flowers had been placed there randomly. He sensed that they were placed there for a purpose…as if someone was trying to tell him something. For some reason, though he couldn't reason why, he felt that the purple and gold lilies had some connection to him. If only he could remember what that connection was. The second reason he had struggled to leave the graveyard behind was Dr. Felton. He knew that Benjamin Felton had a family. From talking to him, he could tell how much they meant to him. Now there he was, lying dead in that graveyard. His death would be unexplained, his family never knowing the events that led to his murder. This fact was haunting Patrick more than he could have anticipated. True, Dr. Felton had once been part of something evil...something for which Patrick could never forgive him. He was once connected to Darden and had bought into his lies. Still, Patrick couldn't help but have sympathy for the man. Patrick believed that, like himself, Felton was caught in the middle of something...a prison from which he couldn't escape. In the end, he had tried to help Patrick. Back at mile marker 224, he had even saved his life. For this, he felt that Benjamin Felton deserved better. Also, Patrick had been comforted by the idea of having someone on his side, someone watching his back. Now he was alone again, up against an unspeakable evil he was only beginning to understand.

Patrick had listened and understood when Felton told him that he couldn't handle things alone. He knew he had no choice but to find someone that would side with him and help him. The only person he could think of was Curtis Flanagan. Recalling his only meeting with Flanagan, this would not have been his first choice. Still, he seemed to be Patrick's only option. During the time he had debated this, he had also thought through another possible scenario…calling the police. While this option was tempting, Patrick also knew that it would be foolish. There were two bodies lying in the cemetery…one who Patrick had shot and killed. How could he explain this to the police without appearing guilty himself? It would only be a matter of time before the police questioned Patrick's identity. How could he explain the tombstone in the graveyard? How would he explain any of this? More importantly was the fact that he may be running out of time. If he still believed his family was out there somewhere, he could not afford to take chances. He even asked himself one more time…"Do you believe they are alive, Patrick?" He quickly decided that yes…he still believed. In the morning he would return to the bar and find Dr. Flanagan.

At the first sign of daylight, Patrick started the Lexus and drove off to find Flanagan. He was able to navigate his way back to the pub, although it wasn't as easy as he had anticipated. Yesterday, when he and Felton had driven to the graveyard, Patrick had slept most of the way. As a result, he lost some valuable time finding his way back to the spot. Finally, Patrick has reached Wilkins, the small street that the pub is located on. He pulls into the lot and sees the familiar tacky, green awning and the clover design above the sign for Murphy's Pub. He drives to the rear of the building, as Felton had done the day before. He parks the Lexus and heads to the same rear door. As was the case the first time, the door is unlocked. Patrick pulls the door open and steps into the into the storage room, negotiating his way around the half-empty boxes of booze. As he enters the bar, he finds it to be in the same condition as he left it, poorly lit and smelling of stale beer and cigarettes. The only thing now missing from the bar is Dr. Flanagan. Patrick notices that the stool Flanagan was sitting on is pulled away from bar. Also absent from the bar is the glass from which Flanagan had been drinking. Patrick calls out for him, "Curtis, are you here?...Curtis, it's Hartley...where are you?" He waits for a response but there is only silence.

Puzzled, he walks around the bar and sees a small pile of broken glass on the floor. Patrick also observes that the pile of broken glass is located right near the telephone. Also, next to the phone is a memo pad and a pencil. It doesn't take him long to deduce that, whatever happened here, someone left in a hurry. It doesn't take long for Patrick to conclude that Curtis must have received a phone call, jotted something down, and left….but what made Curtis drop the beer glass?...who called on the phone? The answer was right there in front of him, although he dreaded even saying the name…"Darden."

Just as the name is beginning to drift through his lips, a noise capture's Patrick's attention…a strange beeping sound coming from somewhere in the bar. He scans the area around him. Soon, he realizes that the sound is emanating from his own pocket…from Felton's cell phone that Patrick had taken from him back in the graveyard. He pulls the phone slowly from his pocket, takes a very deep breath, and answers.

"Well, Mr. Hartley, we finally get a chance to speak." Patrick's hands begin to shake so violently that he must use both to keep from dropping the phone. "I guess this would be you, Darden." The man at the other end of the phone laughs...not just a mere chuckle, but an evil, almost hysterical laugh. "Mr. Hartley, you sound less than pleased. After all we've been through together, I was hoping for a little more enthusiasm." Patrick recognizes this as a mind game...a game he has no intention of playing. "What do you want Darden, what is this all about?" Darden continues to taunt him. "I'm insulted, what makes you think I want something...can't an old friend call another?...I thought we could chat awhile..." Patrick interrupts him..."Did you call Flanagan too?...what did you do to him Darden?" The man makes another noise into the phone...this time something resembling a sigh. "I see that you are in no mood for small-talk, Mr. Hartley, so I'll get right to the point. I think this little game of ours has gone on long enough. You have been a disappointment to me, Hartley. I had very big plans for you...plans for both of us I still intend to see my plan through. Unfortunately, there is still some unfinished business we need to clear up. I have some people here with me. They are people you knew in your former life. These are innocent people who want nothing more than to live. I know you have been to the graveyard, Hartley. Surely you realize that your past life is behind you now. Before Stadnik and Felton became involved, you had put it all behind you. You had a greater purpose…a calling. Look at you now…you are stuck in a life that doesn't want you anymore. Patrick Hartley is dead…Patrick Hartley means nothing in this world. You are much greater than that man." Patrick is unable to stand another minute of this. "Now you listen to me, Darden. If you have my family there with you…and you so much as lay a finger on them…I will hunt you down and kill you myself!" Even when threated, Darden remains calm and once again responds with an evil laugh. "I have no doubt that you are capable of murder, Mr. Hartley. Don't forget, we have been together for a while. I know what you are capable of. You are a man of tremendous strength and perseverance. However, I gave that strength to you. Without me, you are helpless. Worse than that, you are alone now. If you really want to save those you love, your only choice is to give yourself up and leave this life behind. In order to save them, we must bury Patrick Hartley…once and for all."

"Who do you have there with you, Darden? What have you done to them?" With each passing second, Patrick is noticing a different tone in Darden's voice. No longer are questions answered with a laugh. Darden, Patrick senses, is beginning to lose control. "Mr. Hartley, I'm not going to sit on this phone and play twenty questions with you. I am giving you an hour Hartley...one hour to get here. Surely you don't want those you love to die. I had a son once, you know that Hartley? My son...my first-born son Matthew...Matthew Darden. When he was eleven years old he was murdered. His killer was never found. You can't imagine the feeling...losing a child...it makes you hollow, Hartley...to know your child will never have a chance to grow up...never have a chance to become an adult. You don't want to experience that pain do you? Wouldn't you sacrifice your own life to save your child?" Patrick begins to feel nauseous and is growing so dizzy that he can barely stand. "So you have my daughter?...is that what you're telling me?" Darden doesn't answer his question. Instead, he responds by saying..."there is no more time for questions, Hartley. Now is the time for action. Take down this address and be here alone in one hour. It's seven a.m. Hartley. If you are not here by eight a.m. you will find out who I have here with me when you see their lifeless bodies. Do we understand each other?"

After giving Patrick an address, 138 Suffix, along with general directions to its location in Philadelphia, Darden hangs up the phone with one final warning. "Understand Hartley, if you call the police, if you bring anyone with you, our little game is over, and everyone dies." With his heart pounding furiously, Patrick hangs up the phone, folds the piece of paper with the address, and runs out the back door of the pub. He sprints into the parking lot, fumbling in his pocket for the keys to the Lexus. Just as he reaches the door of the vehicle…he sees him. He sees him but it is too late. The man is already at his side, pressing the barrel of a gun to his temple. "Freeze right there, Hartley…or should we call you Darden?"

22

Patrick Hartley closes his eyes tightly and braces himself for what he is certain is coming next...a gunshot to the head. He is certain that the man standing before him is one of Darden's. He lowers his head and prays that the shot will be painless, and it will be over quickly. His only thought is anger. How did he allow himself to be trapped so easily? He realizes now that the call from Darden was merely a trick...a way to draw Patrick outside like a lamb to the slaughter. He tries to focus on his family...praying for just one memory...some hint of recollection so that he can remember their faces before he dies. Such an unfair world, he thinks to himself. What has he done to deserve this? How has he ended up in this dark, hopeless place. A parking lot in a deserted bar is where his life will end…and for what?

After several seconds elapse, Patrick hears no gunshot. Still with dreaded anticipation of what might be to come, he finally opens his eyes. The man standing next to him remains silent for several more seconds, still holding the gun to Patrick's head. Finally, the man speaks. "Stay still Hartley…don't do anything stupid…are you armed?" Still stunned and unable to think clearly, Patrick is at first unable to answer. "Answer me Hartley…do you have a gun?" Patrick moves his eyes in the direction of the Lexus, then answers with a shaky voice…"No…I mean…yes, I have a gun…but it's over there in the car." The man spins Patrick around, grabbing his right arm and pulling it forcefully behind his back. He slams him face-first against the vehicle. "We are going to check for ourselves anyway. Donavon, pat him down for a weapon." Only now does Patrick realize that there is a second man standing a few feet away from him. From the corner of his eye, he is also able to see a white van parked near to where the second man is standing. The second man walks over to Patrick and runs his hands down his midsection, then down his leg, and to his socks. "Yep he's clean" the man says to his partner. The man with the gun spins Hartley around to face him. The man appears to be in his thirties. He is not what you would call a large man, but seems to be built rock-solid, as if he was carved from granite. He is wearing dark-colored clothing and has a slightly scarred complexion. Aside from this, there is nothing about this man that strikes Patrick, except that he somehow looks familiar.

Patrick is still standing with his back to the Lexus. The two men stand side-by-side, facing him. They seem to be studying him…waiting for him to make a move. The second man is much older, probably in his mid to late fifties. In contrast to his partner, this man's build is anything but solid. He is short and chubby, probably around five foot six. He has a sloppy, unshaven appearance and wears faded blue jeans and a torn bomber jacket. Also in contrast to his partner, he doesn't look the slightest bit familiar to Patrick.

After what seems like an eternity, the man with the gun finally speaks. "Jesus Hartley, what the hell are you thinking running around out here without a gun?" At first, Patrick can only stare back at him, the confusion of the moment rendering him speechless. Finally, he gathers himself enough to speak. "I…I don't know…what is going on here?...who are you people?...how do you know me?" The man with the gun shoots a quick glance at his partner, then back to Patrick. "You still don't remember anything, do you Hartley? Although I can tell by that look in your eye that you kind of remember me. Don't worry, we are not with Darden and we are not here to hurt you. In fact, we may be the only chance you have left." Patrick shakes his head, as if in disbelief. "You look familiar to me, but I don't…I can't remember where I've seen you. Please…tell me why you're here. I don't have much time left. Darden has given me only one hour. He says I have to go to him…he says he has my family…he says he'll kill them if I don't get there in time." The man with the gun places his hand on Patrick's shoulder. "Alright Hartley…alright…slow down for a second…Darden called you here?...how did he know you were here?" Patrick begins to grow increasingly impatient. He imagines a ticking clock in his head, every second ticking closer to the deadline. He has no time to waste. "I don't think he knows I'm here. He called me on Benjamin Felton's cell phone…Darden's people killed Felton…they know I picked up his phone…Darden gave me an address." Patrick reaches into his pocket and hands the piece of paper to the man with the gun. The man quickly scans the address, then hands the paper off to his partner as he starts talking. "Ok , listen to me Hartley. This place isn't far from here. It's only going to take us about twenty minutes or so. We are only going to get one shot at this, so we have to do it right…" Patrick interrupts him, "Who are you people?...why should I trust you?"

The one with the gun steps closer to Patrick, grabbing him by the collar and holding him forcefully against the Lexus. "You have no choice but to trust us Hartley. Now, if you have any sense at all you will shut up and let me explain. Are you ready to listen?" With eyes wide with terror, Patrick nods his head. "Okay then" the man continues, "my name is David O'Dell and that is Lou Donavon. You don't need to know who we work for, only why we are here. We have been watching you a long time, Hartley. That's why I knew enough to call you by your project name…Matthew Darden. You recognize me because you have seen me before. You have been close to me…closer than you realize. You stood just a couple of feet from me in a bathroom in Atlantic City…right before you knocked off one of Darden's enemies…Rico Satori." Patrick shakes his head in denial. "No, you're lying…I didn't do that…I'm not a murderer!" O'Dell reaches out and grabs Patrick forcefully by the arm. "Listen to me Hartley…I saw you…I was there…my partner over there was in that bathroom also and he saw you. Patrick Hartley is not a murderer, but Matthew Darden was. You were Matthew Darden, you just don't remember. We have been watching you for a long time. You saw me watching you, that's why I look so familiar to you. You saw me outside of your apartment in Wildwood…The Ocean Winds Apartments. Do you remember the apartment?" Patrick stares back at him blankly. "Maybe this will help spark your memory."

O'Dell reaches into the pocket of his dark pants and produces a folded piece of white paper. As he hands it over to Patrick, he explains its meaning. "We printed this off the computer in that apartment. There were dozens of writings just like these on the hard drive. We can only assume you wrote them. Think hard Hartley and try to remember. What inspired you to write this?...what were you thinking then?...what did you know?" Patrick unfolds the piece of paper and begins to read what is written on the page...

The mindless humans bathe in the warm, inviting darkness...unaware of the heartless and savage creatures swimming among them...

"You're saying I wrote this? This means nothing to me...I don't remember ever writing this. We are wasting time here. Don't you understand...I need to get to Darden. I told you what he said he would do to my family if I don't get there in time..." Patrick's hands are shaking uncontrollably now. He is beginning to unravel again. "Ever since I first met Dr. Stadnik, I have tried to remember. Stadnik told me that memories would return in time. He told me that it would all come back to me eventually. Why can't I remember?" Patrick slides down the Lexus and falls to the ground sobbing. "I can't do this anymore...I can't take any more of this... I can't even remember my own family... Who knows if they are even alive...I don't know what is real any more…it feels like I'm in a nightmare and I can't wake up…when you first snuck up on me and put that gun to my head…I was afraid…but part of me was relieved because…because I thought then at least it would just be over." Patrick places his elbows on his knees and cups his hands over his face. "I'm tired, can you understand that?…I'm just so tired."

O'Dell crouches down to speak to Hartley. He lowers his voice to calm him. "Listen, to me…there is a lot at stake here. This guy Darden represents the worst kind of evil. Whatever he has planned, you can rest assured that it is deadly. From what we can tell, he has had a plan all along. He has been one step ahead of us the whole time. Obviously, you are an important part of his plan…you are probably the final piece of his plan. For whatever reason, he can't move forward without you. We can't let him win…whatever the risks…regardless of our own lives…we can't let him win. As far as your family goes, you should know that your daughter is in fact alive. I can say that for certain because I saw her myself." Patrick removes his hands from his eyes and looks up at O'Dell. "You saw my daughter?…when?"

"Your daughter is with a woman by the name of Beverly Holloway. She is the mother of an attorney from Philadelphia, Anna Holloway." Patrick interrupts, "I know about Anna Holloway. She was killed on her way home from work..." Odell continues, "That's correct, and we suspected that Anna was connected to all of this and we have recently found out how. Anna Holloway represented a client by the name of Thomas Van Allen on an extortion charge. Mr. Van Allen was also linked to international terrorism and was closely connected to Darden. Van Allen was eventually shot outside of a convenience store. Does that sound familiar to you Hartley?" Patrick is afraid to answer. "Yes, but only because Stadnik told me about Van Allen. You aren't saying I killed him too...I told you...I'm not a killer!" "O'Dell stands back up and looks down at Patrick. "I'm not saying it was you. We don't know who killed Van Allen. From what we know, he had countless enemies, but Darden was one of them. Anyway, what we do know is this...in the process of representing him, Anna Holloway found out much more than she should have. This may also explain why she somehow became connected with your wife. For reasons that aren't yet clear to us, your wife left your daughter in the care of Anna

Holloway. It seems that your wife was aware that she was in danger. Therefore, your daughter was in danger as well. She needed someone she could trust…someone who knew what she was up against. We're not sure what happened to your wife, but we must assume the worst. Somehow, she knew Darden was after her. She must have thought it was only a matter of time before he found her and your daughter. This is the only explanation we can come up with as to why she entrusted the Holloways with your daughter's care. Anyway, I was able to contact Beverly Holloway and we attempted to warn her. You need to understand that, at the time, this was all we could do. We knew that Darden's people were close by and we couldn't risk blowing our cover. Unfortunately, Beverly Holloway must not have gotten out in time. It makes sense that Darden probably has them now. Patrick brushes the tears from his eyes, climbs to his feet, and stares at O'Dell and Donovan. "Then let's go get my daughter back."

23

The three men decided they would take two separate vehicles. O'Dell and Donavon would lead in the white van and Patrick would follow in the Lexus. O'Dell had insisted on this approach and there was no time to argue. The time when they left the parking lot of Murphy's Pub was 7:21am. O'Dell had estimated that the drive to the address on Suffix would take approximately twenty minutes. This would leave few precious moments as is. If Patrick was to bicker about details, they surely wouldn't make it on time. Patrick had also decided that, although he knew very little about the two men, he had no choice but to trust them. Darden had stated that eight a.m. was the deadline and the three men knew enough to believe him.

As Patrick drove down the highway, following closely behind the white van in front of him, he was lost in deep thought. His mind was spinning in seemingly a thousand different directions. The rainstorm from the previous evening had long since moved on, replaced by a perfectly clear and blue morning sky. Despite the weather, Patrick sensed that there was a storm of another kind brewing on the horizon in front of them. His stomach was tied in knots of fear for the unknown. In the moments of quiet while driving…the calm before the inevitable storm…he tried his best to prepare himself for what was lying ahead. There seemed to be so many questions…who were O'Dell and Donavon?…what were their motives?…they say they didn't work for Darden…could he really trust them?…could he afford not to? The other question was that of timing. Why would Darden try to lure Patrick to the address on Suffix in broad daylight? This seemed to be a big risk for the man to be taking. If he thought there was any chance of a violent confrontation, why in the daylight? Surely it would be more likely that someone might see or hear something in the daylight as opposed to in the cover of darkness. As Patrick thought about this further, it started to make more sense to him. Perhaps the location they were headed to is some place so remote that the risk of being seen or heard would be minimal. Perhaps Darden felt that he would gain an advantage in the daylight. After all, the light would give him the benefit of clear site. It would make it possible for Darden to ensure that Patrick was indeed alone. Darden may also have reason to believe that there would be no confrontation. Perhaps he believed that Patrick would have no choice but to cooperate. If the man was indeed holding Patrick's daughter, this would be all the leverage he would need.

Patrick continues to tail the white van as it turns off Washington Boulevard and on to a street called Jefferson. They are now in the middle of a very run-down neighborhood. Patrick takes notice of the dilapidated houses, graffiti-covered sidewalks, and abandoned vehicles lining the shoulder of the road. Although obviously a very dangerous part of town, it is also eerily quiet and empty this time of morning. O'Dell pulls the white van to the side of the road and Patrick follows in the Lexus. O'Dell had explained to Patrick that they would turn off well before they reached Suffix. This way, they stood a better chance of not being seen together by Darden or his men. It is here that the three of them would stop and formulate their plan. As O'Dell and Donavon climb out of the van, Patrick parks the Lexus and steps out onto the sidewalk. The three men take in the crumbled neighborhood around them. "Jesus", O'Dell remarks, "it looks like there has been a war here. I'd hate to wind up here on a dark night...alright, let's talk about how this is going to work. Hartley, Darden thinks you are coming alone...." O'Dell looks down at his wristwatch. "It is now 7:42am, so we don't have much time. The turnoff for Suffix is just down the road about a mile. The address you have written down here is 138. Now listen Hartley, I don't really know what to expect here but you're going to have to trust us...Darden didn't bring you here to kill you. He has other plans for you...he needs you. What we need you to do is stall him while Donavon and I find another way in."

Patrick's pulse is racing, and he begins to feel light-headed and queasy. "That's it...that's the plan?...I'm just supposed to walk right up to him?" For the first time, Donavon speaks. " Look Hartley, that's all we have right now. If Darden sees you with us, that's the end. If he does have your daughter, he will kill her…do you understand? The only chance we have is to surprise him. Here, take this and put it in your sock." Donavon pulls out a small handgun from his jacket pocket. "Don't pull the gun unless you absolutely have to….and not before we get there. It all comes down to this, Hartley. This is the chance you have been waiting for. We won't get another…you only have a few minutes left…you need to go now."

It takes Patrick less than four minutes to reach the address on Suffix. He stands at the mailbox which displays the address…138 Suffix. In front of him is a gravel driveway which leads down to a small, old house. Surrounding the house are several large pine trees. The home looks to be abandoned except for two vehicles parked at the bottom of the driveway. The vehicle closest to the house is a red pickup truck, the one behind it a silver Audi. Patrick recognizes the Audi from his first visit to Murphy's Pub when he and Felton had gone see Curtis Flanagan. Patrick can now only assume that Darden has Curtis also. Did Curtis drive to the house? If so…why? Patrick then remembers the broken glass on the floor of the pub.

He is even more convinced that his earlier suspicion had been correct. Flanagan must have received a phone call from Darden, Still, he wonders what motivated Curtis to drive here. Surely it wasn't because of Patrick's daughter. What did Darden have on Curtis? Patrick has no idea what the answer is...but he has a feeling he is about to find out.

Although he has no wristwatch to measure the time, Patrick knows that it must be closing in on the 8am deadline. He cannot afford to delay any longer and begins his descent down the gravel driveway to the old house. With each step, he begins to sweat more profusely....not due to heat or fatigue...but just plain fear....not a fear for his own safety...a fear of failure. He is aware that any wrong move from this point forward could mean disaster. He reminds himself to stay alert. Finally, he is just a few steps away from the front door. He pauses and looks over his shoulder, half expecting someone to sneak up on him at any moment. For several seconds he stands still but sees or hears nothing. He is unsure what to do...his feet frozen underneath him as if he is standing on an iceberg. Just then, something grabs his attention...a flicker of light.

The source of the flickering is the porch
light. Someone inside the house turns the light on
and off again several times…as if summoning
Patrick to come forth. With a long, deep breath
Patrick steps forward onto the porch. He takes a
final look over his shoulder, then steps forward
again and reaches for the front door handle. Before
his hand can reach it, the door opens suddenly,
sending him back-peddling. He regains his balance
and investigates the open doorway. He sees no one,
only an empty staircase leading to the upstairs of
the house. He then hears a voice calling to him.
"Come inside slowly Hartley and close the door
behind you…keep your hands where I can see
them." Patrick closes the door and walks slowly
into the living room, keeping his arms outstretched
as instructed. When he enters the living room, he
sees a man sitting in an armchair and staring in his
direction. The man appears to be in his mid-to-late
fifties, with very thin white hair, and a white
mustache which curls slightly at both ends. He is
dressed in a grey flannel shirt and blue jeans.
Although he appears to be of average size, he sits
low in the chair, making him look small and
awkward.

"Mr. Hartley, I'm so glad you could join us. It's been a long time. I see you've come alone, so you've passed the first test. You can rest assured that I'm not alone, however. It would not be in your best interest to try anything foolish." The man then calls into the next room. "Joseph, would you be so kind as to come in here and check our guest?" Another man quickly enters the room. He is also dressed in blue jeans but is much younger. Unlike the older man, he is a husky, burly man in his twenties. He wears a tight-fitting grey t-shirt which shows off his muscular build. The man also carries a handgun, which he hands off to the older man as he passes by. The younger man approaches Patrick and grabs him by the back of the neck with his right hand. He pushes Patrick forward, driving him face-first onto the hardwood floor. The impact with the floor pushes Patrick's nose to his face, causing him to wince in pain. His nose begins to bleed profusely, and he begins to taste the blood as it runs down into his mouth. "Joseph, take it easy on our guest. We don't want to appear rude, do we?" The muscled man stands over Patrick and begins to pat the pockets of his pants, then runs his hands down each leg. Patrick's pulse quickens as he remembers the small handgun tucked into his sock.

Fortunately, he has been pushed to the ground in such a way that the gun is under the front of his leg. The man searching him is unable to detect the weapon. Satisfied that he is unarmed, the man grabs him by the back of shirt and pulls him to his feet. The older man rises from the chair now, pulls a white handkerchief from his pocket, and hands it to Patrick. "Clean yourself up now." Patrick uses the handkerchief to wipe the blood from his nose. Despite his deep gasps for breath, he feels like he is suffocating and is unable to speak. "Sorry that my men can be a bit rough. You see, they are very protective of me. Now that I have your attention, let's begin. Since it appears you are not able to speak for now, I will start. First, you should know that I never blamed you, Mr. Hartley. Despite the rather abrupt greeting you received here, I am not angry with you. You were always a good soldier. That is until Stadnik and Felton became involved. Fortunately, we don't have to worry about either of them any longer. Then again, you already know this. I don't feel a bit of remorse for what has happened to them and you shouldn't either. They chose to cross me, Mr. Hartley. When they did that, they wrote a check they were not able to cash. The strong survive and the weak die. You are still alive, Mr. Hartley. You are still alive because you are the strongest of the strong…the best of the best. My people told me what you did to one of my men back at the cemetery…one bullet, Mr. Hartley…that's all you needed was one bullet…and you hit your target with a chest shot…directly in the heart…through bushes…that's very impressive. How do you think you did that, Mr. Hartley?…you did that because I showed you how to do that."

Patrick removes the handkerchief from his nose and has finally regained control of his breathing. "I don't understand any of this…who are you?…where is my daughter?" The older man raises his hand in a motion to silence Patrick. "Let's slow down, Hartley. I assure you that your questions will be answered. Let's take it one at a time though. In answer to your first question, I'm a little insulted that you don't remember who I am. Don't worry though, it's understandable given the circumstances so I won't hold it against you. My name, of course, is Dr. Owen Darden. Even though you don't remember me now, you will in time. We will continue right where we left off and this unpleasantness will be forgotten. As for your daughter, Mr. Hartley, this is one of the many small details we can't allow ourselves to be concerned with. We are on the verge of a breakthrough, Mr. Hartley…one of the greatest achievements in human history. What was once just a dream for me has become a very reachable goal. The history of the world is about to change, and I am inviting you to be a part of this wonderful transformation. We have made some enormous sacrifices along the way. Yours will be to leave your old life behind and move on. There can be no other way, Mr. Hartley.

As Patrick tries to process and make some sense of all this information, he only grows more confused. He is clear on only one fact. Although he has just now officially learned that the older man is Darden, he knew it from the time he laid eyes on him. He had remembered the man, although his brain had probably wanted him to forget. He remembers how he feared him and how unpredictable he was. Dr. Darden might be insane, but he is also very intelligent and highly capable. When Darden says the history of the world is about to change, Patrick believes him. Then, another thought comes to Patrick…where the hell are O'Dell and Donavon? By his best estimate, he has been in the house for close to ten minutes. How long is he supposed to be able to stall? Shouldn't the two men have found a back way in by now? Maybe they have already tried and failed. Patrick's only hope is to stall a little while longer. "Listen Darden, I don't know who you think I am…I only know that…I mean…I am Patrick Hartley…I am just a man…just a normal man who wants a normal life. I had a family…I had a wife and daughter. Whatever it is you have planned, I want no part of it. Give me back my daughter…let us go our way and you can go on yours." His attempt at reasoning with Darden is met only with laughter. "Hartley, how nice of you…you will let me go on my way…wonderfully entertaining. As much as I'd love to hear more, we have a schedule to keep. You will go with Joseph now. He will take you downstairs. What I can promise you is that your re-transformation will be relatively painless. Tomorrow, you will awaken and none of this will matter anymore. As I said before, we will pick up exactly where we left off. We've all made sacrifices, Mr. Hartley. Now it is time that you made yours." Darden then turns to the younger man and hands him back the gun. "Joseph, please take this and escort Mr. Hartley downstairs. Oh, and Joseph…please try not to kill him unless he does something stupid. Mr. Hartley, we will talk again in the morning. This will be a much different conversation then."

Joseph walks behind Patrick and presses the barrel of the handgun to the base of his skull. He orders Patrick forward with a shove and just one word…"MOVE". He walks Patrick past Darden, who has already turned to walk back to the chair he had been sitting in. They walk across the living room and the man guides Patrick to the staircase heading downstairs. Patrick knows that his time is running out, but he has no idea what his next move should be. To attempt to draw the weapon now, with Joseph holding a gun to his head, would be suicide. If he doesn't do it now, he might not get another chance. Although he knows he is running out of options, he can't muster up the will to draw his weapon. They have reached the top of the staircase…Patrick senses that the journey is over, and he has lost.

Just then from the basement…a popping sound. The one popping sound is followed by a second…now a third. After the third pop, a sound of shouting. Joseph stops pushing Patrick forward and removes the gun from against his head. He points the gun down the stairs just as a man is rounding the corner...David O'Dell. Patrick's eyes meet O'Dell's for a split second. O'Dell shouts to Patrick. "Hartley, get down!" O'Dell then begins to fire just as Joseph does. Patrick watches in horror as O'Dell is struck by a bullet just below the left side of his chest. Joseph is also struck, and blood splatters from his head and onto Patrick's shirt. Joseph drops the gun to the floor at the top of the stairs. Patrick struggles to gain control of the weapon. Unfortunately, the weight of the large man falling on top of Patrick forces him down the staircase. The two men roll down several steps before Patrick can recover his balance and reaches for the gun in his sock. To his horror, he mishandles the weapon and it slips through his fingertips. Patrick watches in what seems like slow motion as the gun bounces down the staircase. Just as he turns to start back up the stairs, he sees Darden looking down at him. Darden reaches the gun that Joseph dropped...and is pointing it right at Patrick. Patrick hears the gun in Darden's hand go off just as he hears someone rounding the bend at the bottom of the staircase. The man at the bottom of the staircase shouts..."Hartley, No!" Patrick recognizes the voice to be Donavon's. His warning is a fraction of a second too late. Patrick feels the cold metal of the bullet puncture his flesh. There is very little pain…it's as if he is not falling, but floating…floating into darkness.

24

Patrick feels as if he is no longer surrounded by darkness. Instead, he is suddenly immersed in a warm, white light. A calm settles over him as he feels the light lifting him gently upward. He feels as if he has been become detached from his own body and has the sensation of looking down from above. He is slowly lifted from the staircase and floats along, first to the top of the stairs, and then out the front door of the old house. He is outside now, floating above the trees in the front yard and starting up the gravel driveway. The front yard of the house is not as he remembers it, however. The vehicles are gone from the driveway and the gravel path is surrounded on both sides by row after row of beautiful flowers...purple and gold lilies. As he stares down and marvels at this beautiful display, he also sees a woman and a young girl. Both are wearing pretty, yellow sundresses. They are smiling now and waving up to him. The little girl prances through the flowers, her arms stretched out as if pretending to be an airplane. Patrick notices that the girl's steps neither trample nor wilt the lovely flowers. It's as if the girl is floating, her small footsteps remaining just slightly off the ground. He turns his attention to the woman now, who smiles in delight as she watches the little girl at play. The woman looks to be perfectly at peace, and she too appears to be floating next to the child. As Patrick looks down at them, he is captivated by the beauty of the woman and child. He smiles back at them, waving his arm frantically, trying to reach them. His smile fades as he realizes he can't reach them. The woman stares up at him and begins to whisper something. Patrick focuses on her mouth, trying to read her lips. He can hear her words now, a single phrase the woman whispers repeatedly. "Come back to us Patrick…come back to us Patrick. Now in panic, he tries again to use his arms to draw himself closer…but the white light begins to push him even higher now. He can still hear the woman pleading…"come back to us Patrick…please don't leave us." Slowly, the woman and child fade away from view until all he can see is the white light.

Strangely, though he can no longer see her, the woman's voice grows louder. He can hear her more clearly now, although he can still only see the white light. "Patrick, wake up…please Patrick…please come back to us. Slowly, the white light begins to fade, and Patrick can see the woman and child again. This time, their faces are directly in front of him, just a few feet away. He no longer feels like he is floating. Instead, the two faces are above him now. He stares at them intently and tries his best to absorb every detail, fearing that they may soon disappear forever. The woman's hair is a beautiful blonde color, and her bright green eyes sparkle like emeralds. The young girl is equally as pretty, her hair so golden that it reminds him of the gold lilies on which she danced. Her face, so smooth and perfect…like an angel. The girl looks down at him and says something that makes Patrick believe he must be dreaming. "Daddy, you're back!"

As if struck by a lightning bolt, the words send a current through Patrick. He realizes that he is no longer dreaming. He looks up at the little girl and, before he even realizes what he is about to say, speaks her name…"Sarah." He then turns to the woman and says, "Kimberly." The woman and child stare back at him with warm smiles on their faces. Patrick slowly begins to come to and turns his head to look around. He now sees that he is in a hospital room, surrounded by beeping monitors. An IV drips fluid into the back of his right hand, and small wires are taped to his bare chest. The woman and child move off to the side as a nurse and doctor enter the room. Patrick hears Kimberly address the doctor, a nervous excitement in her voice. "He…he's awake!…he's awake and he remembers!"

Patrick immediately recognizes the doctor…Curtis Flanagan. Flanagan turns to the woman and child…"Ok, you'll need to step outside for a minute. You'll be able to come back in soon I promise." Dr. Flanagan stands over Patrick and speaks to him directly. "Hartley, it's Curtis Flanagan, do you know where you are?" Still groggy and confused, Patrick shakes his head. "You're at Temple University Neuroscience Center. You've been asleep for almost four days now. You were treated for a bullet wound to your abdomen. You are going to make it, Hartley." Patrick's lips are parched, and he is barely able to speak. He can only utter a single word…"Darden." Flanagan places his hand on top of Patrick's and smiles. "Darden is dead, Hartley. Thanks to you, my brother-in-law Mitch is still alive and so am I. You did good Hartley…you did good. As for your family, you already know that they are alive and well. The best news is that you remember them. Remember what I told you about my work with the chemical Citicoline? That's the chemical used to treat victims of head trauma. Its working well for you. That's why you recognize them. What do you say we bring them back in here? There's also someone else with them who wants to thank you." Before Patrick can say anything, Flanagan walks out the door of the hospital room and returns seconds later, followed by three smiling people. The first is Patrick's wife Kimberly, followed immediately by his daughter Sarah. The third person, Patrick doesn't recognize. She introduces herself as Beverly Holloway, the mother of Anna Holloway. Beverly steps over to the bed, leans down, and kisses Patrick gently on the forehead. "I know we've never met, Patrick, but I feel like I know you. Thank you so much for helping to save my life." Beverly then hugs Kimberly, who whispers to her softly…"thank you Beverly…you will always be part of our family." Then, Beverly bends down and hugs little Sarah. She sobs as she speaks to the child. "As for you little one…I'm going to come and visit you often…don't you grow up too fast little angel." She then turns back to Patrick and says, "it's time for me to leave the three of you alone to get reacquainted…you have a lot of catching up to do. Come on Dr. Flanagan, let me buy you a cup of coffee." With that, Beverly Holloway and Dr. Curtis Flanagan leave the room. Finally, it is just the three of them. The woman and child stand there smiling at him. Patrick Hartley has been reborn.

25

Patrick rocks slowly back and forth in the comfortable, blue living room chair. He relishes every moment of the wonderful peace and quiet. Although his memory hasn't yet returned completely, he can't imagine ever being happier. He takes such pleasure in each day spent with Kimberly and young Sarah. Sarah is adjusting well to her new life. She seems almost completely unaffected by the trauma she has endured. Patrick has also discovered that she is quite a talented artist for her age. He can spend hours watching her as she draws beautiful scenes with her colored pencils. Her favorite things to draw are rainbows…fabulous, perfectly colored rainbows. Earlier in the evening. Little Sarah had informed Patrick and Kimberly that she was going up to her room to "draw daddy the best picture ever." Her words were like music to Patrick's ears.

Meanwhile, Kimberly is deeply engrossed in another one of her spy novels. She sits on the couch with her bare feet resting on the coffee table, eyes locked on the pages in front of her. Patrick takes the opportunity to study her from across the room. He thinks to himself how lucky is to have her. How was he ever able to survive without her and Sarah?

Not quite a month has passed since Patrick's release from Temple University Hospital. The Hartley family has settled into a wonderful routine of quiet evenings at their new home in King of Prussia, PA. The location of the new home was chosen with the help of their new friend, Beverly Holloway. On her last visit to the hospital just before Patrick's release, she had mentioned that the home across the street from her was going up for sale. The home had been owned by Larry Mitchell, a long-time neighbor and friend of the Holloways. The timing couldn't have been more perfect. Patrick and Kimberly had just been discussing where they should look for a place to settle down and begin anew. They had both agreed that they needed to find a nice house in a safe neighborhood. Also, they needed to arrange for someone to look after Sarah when they started back to work. Beverly was more than happy to volunteer for the job and little Sarah could not have been more pleased. Not that either of them would have to start back to work anytime soon. Thanks to a substantial check from the government that the family had received upon Patrick's release from the hospital, there would be no financial worries anytime soon.

The check had been delivered by a man who works for David O'Dell. He introduced himself simply as John and refused to give a last name. He explained to Patrick that the money was to compensate him for his pain and suffering. In exchange, Patrick would agree to remain quiet about Owen Darden and anything related to the matter. This request was delivered to Patrick in a manner that made it clear to him that it was in his best interest to comply. During the visit, this mysterious man John also filled him in on some missing details of that fateful night at the old house. He informed Patrick that David O'Dell was still in the hospital being treated for a near-fatal gunshot wound. Apparently, the bullet had struck him just three inches below his heart. Although he will be in for a very long recovery, O'Dell is expected to pull through. As for Donavon, the man who ended up fatally shooting Owen Darden, he was not so fortunate. Seconds before shooting Darden, Donavon himself suffered a bullet wound in the back from one of Darden's men. The bullet penetrated his lung and he would pass away on the way to the hospital. This was jarring news to Patrick because this was the man who had saved his life. Without the heroic efforts of O'Dell and Donavon, he would not be here today.

As for Owen Darden, Patrick was told that much of what the man was up to would remain classified. He was informed that the old house is still being searched, and items that have been discovered there show the magnitude of what Darden had planned. Patrick wasn't given many specifics but was told everything from a detailed layout of major airports. Military bases, and even sports venues have been recovered from the house. In addition, a list of names ranking from the President of the United States to high-ranking officials from all over the world were discovered. One thing is for certain, the world is a much safer place now that Owen Darden is no longer in it.

Patrick pulls himself up from the blue chair and walks over to Kimberly, still sitting on the sofa. He sits down beside her and gently touches her hand. Kimberly turns to Patrick and smiles, placing the novel she has been reading down on her lap. "There's something I never asked you," Patrick says to her. "I never asked you about the flowers...the purple and gold lilies...what does it mean?" Kimberly laughs warmly before answering him. "I'm sure you don't remember this so I'm going to tell you the story. For our first wedding anniversary, you came home with a bouquet of flowers for me...purple and gold lilies. I joked with you that, although the bouquet was beautiful, you obviously didn't know much about flowers. I told you that you usually only see purple and gold lilies at funerals because they symbolize life and death. Without hesitating, you said that's why you chose them...because you will love me every day of this life...and still love me after we've moved on. I never forgot those words...that was the best thing anyone has ever said to me. Ever since then, purple and gold lilies have been my favorite flowers. I never stopped thinking about that day...even in the worst of times...after your accident...when I had to leave Sarah with Anna Holloway....when I knew it was only a matter of time before they found me. I placed those flowers at your gravesite. Even then, I believed that you would find them and know I was out there somewhere...waiting for you to find me."

Kimberly begins to sob quietly. Patrick places his hand on the back of her shoulder to comfort her. "I was scared, Patrick...I was so scared...being held prisoner by that...madman. But even then, I thought about what you said to me on our first anniversary. I knew that even if you were dead...and even if I was going to be killed as well...I knew you would be there waiting for me on the other side...that's what got me through the worst of times. Patrick takes Kimberly's hand again, leans over, and kisses her gently on the forehead. "Wow, I guess I'm a romantic after all." Kimberly laughs as she wipes away her tears. "Don't flatter yourself, Patrick Hartley...but yes, you really are a romantic." Patrick grips her hand tighter now. "Promise me we'll never be apart again." Kimberly touches him softly on the side of his face. "You are never getting rid of me."

Little Sarah Hartley lies on her bed and stares up at the ceiling fan, intently watching the slow spin of the fan's blades. The comforter which he lays on is a pink Cinderella design, with matching pink pillows. The window curtains are also decorated in honor of this, her favorite fairy tale. Colored pencils are scattered about the bed and bedroom floor around her. Across the room on the child's little work desk sits the picture she promised to draw for her father. Instead of her usual brightly colored rainbows, this picture is entirely different. The picture she has drawn is the smiling face of a man…an older man with thin gray hair and a moustache that curls at both ends. Sarah, still on the bed, crosses her arms tightly around her own shoulders. Rocking back and forth, she repeats to herself…"please make it stop…please make the itching go away."

ABOUT THE AUTHOR

Brad was born and raised in Pittsburgh, Pennsylvania. He is an avid reader of books and is a self-described action movie buff. He enjoys travel, music, and the company of family and friends.

For more information about the **Darden Pursuit** please visit:

https://sites.google.com/site/thedardenpursuit/

Made in the USA
Middletown, DE
05 April 2019